ROBOT RIOT!

911300

D1080624

Also by Andy Griffiths

ANDY GRIFFITHS
ROBOT RIOT!

MARION LLOYD BOOKS

First published in the UK in 2010 by
Marion Lloyd Books
An imprint of Scholastic Ltd
Euston House, 24 Eversholt Street
London, NW1 1DB, UK
Registered office: Westfield Road, Southam, Warwickshire, CV47 0RA
SCHOLASTIC and associated logos are trademarks and/or registered
trademarks of Scholastic Inc.

Copyright © Andy Griffiths, 2009
First published in Australia by Pan Macmillan Australia Pty Ltd, 2009
The right of Andy Griffiths to be identified as the author of this
work has been asserted by him.

ISBN 978 1407 10901 5

A CIP catalogue record for this book is available
from the British Library

All rights reserved
This book is sold subject to the condition that it
shall not, by way of trade or otherwise, be lent, hired out or otherwise
circulated in any form of binding or cover other than that in which it is
published. No part of this publication may be reproduced, stored in a
retrieval system, or transmitted in any form or by any means
(electronic, mechanical, photocopying, recording or otherwise)
without the prior written permission of
Scholastic Limited.

Printed in the UK by CPI Bookmarque, Croydon, CR0 4TD
Papers used by Scholastic Children's Books are made from wood
grown in sustainable forests.

1 3 5 7 9 10 8 6 4 2

This is a work of fiction. Names, characters, places, incidents
and dialogues are products of the author's imagination or are used
fictitiously. Any resemblance to actual people, living or dead,
events or locales is entirely coincidental.

www.scholastic.co.uk/zone

For Mr Bechervaise

BRENT LIBRARIES	
91130000025560	
PETERS	23-Feb-2010
£5.99	BREAL
CF	

Chapter 1

Once upon a time

Once upon a time there was – and still is – a school called Northwest Southeast Central School.

Northwest Southeast Central School is located to the south-east of a town called Northwest, which is located to the north-west of a big city called Central City.

You don't need to know where Central City is, because it's not important. What *is* important is the school. In this school there is a classroom. And in that classroom there is a year five class. Most important of all, in that class of year five students there is a student named Henry McThrottle who likes telling stories.

That's where I come in.

I'm Henry McThrottle . . . and this is my latest story.

Chapter 2

A new recruit

It all started one morning at school. I was out in the playground with my friends Jenny Friendly, Jack Japes, Gretel Armstrong and Newton Hooton. We were with the rest of our class, picking up rubbish.

Thief, the dog that always hangs around the school, was also there. But Thief wasn't trying to pick up rubbish. He was trying to *eat* it.

"Eeeuuww, yuck!" said Jenny, as Thief chomped into an old, dried-up sandwich covered in dirt.

"Look on the bright side," said Jack. "It's one less piece of rubbish that *we* have to pick up."

"I wish he would eat paper and plastic containers as well," said Gretel, bending over to pick up an empty bottle. "I'm *so* tired of picking up rubbish."

"I don't see why we have to pick up rubbish anyway," said Jack.

"We *have* to pick up rubbish," explained Jenny, "because if we don't, Northwest Southeast Central School won't win the Northwest Tidiest School Award."

"Who cares?" said Jack.

"I do," replied Jenny, "because Mr Greenbeard cares, and if we don't win, he's going to be really upset. And I don't like to see anybody upset."

"What about me?" said Jack. "I'm upset about having to pick up rubbish. I came to school to learn how to be a cartoonist, not a bin man!"

"And what about the germs?" said Newton, trembling. "Rubbish has lots of germs, and I'm scared of them!"

This was not surprising. Newton was scared of pretty much everything.

"I've told you before, Newton," said Jenny, patting him on the arm. "You don't have to be scared of germs. Just wash your hands with warm water and soap when we're finished and you'll be fine."

"No, he won't!" said Jack. "It doesn't work."

"Yes, he *will*," said Jenny. "My mother says warm water and soap kills all germs."

"Maybe," said Jack, "but think about it! You turn the tap on with your germy hands and afterwards you turn the tap off with your clean hands, but the germs that you left on the tap when you turned it on with your germy hands get back on your clean hands and make them all germy again, and then when you're least expecting it – probably when you're asleep – the germs creep up your arms . . . and on to your neck . . . and then they ooze up your chin . . . into your mouth . . . and then down your throat and—"

"Jack!" Jenny and I both said at the same time.

"What?" he said.

"You're scaring Newton!"

Newton was shaking violently and gulping for air. I put my arm around his shoulders until he got his breathing back under control.

"It's not my fault," said Jack. "I didn't *invent* germs."

"No one's saying you did," said Jenny. "But you *are* going on and on about them."

"Sorry, Newton," said Jack. "I just hate picking up rubbish. It makes me crazy. And all because our headmaster wants to win a stupid award . . . I'd like to tell him exactly what I think of him and his stupid old award!"

"Looks like you're about to get your chance," said Gretel, "because here he comes!"

We turned to look.

Mr Greenbeard was striding across the playground.

He was wearing a white naval-style uniform, like the captain of a ship might wear.

And there was a good reason for this.

As far as Mr Greenbeard is concerned, he *is* the captain of a ship, and the staff and students of Northwest Southeast Central School are his crew. I know it sounds crazy, but he's not actually crazy. He's just crazy about ships and sailing.

He had a girl with him who I didn't recognize. She had short brown hair and intense, staring eyes.

We all stood to attention and saluted.

Mr Greenbeard returned our salute.

"Good morning, 5B!" he said. "You're doing a wonderful job on the decks here. Keep this up and we'll have the old tub shipshape in no time! I'm very pleased to announce that we have a new recruit to assist us in our grand endeavour." Mr Greenbeard looked around. "Where's your commanding officer?"

"Mr Brainfright?" said David Worthy, our class captain.

"Yes, he *is* your commanding officer, isn't he?"

"Yes, sir," said David, proudly. "He left me in charge."

"And me," said Fiona McBrain, looking a little peeved. "I am *co*-class captain, you know."

"Sorry," mumbled David. "I mean, he left *us* in charge."

"Yes, but where is he?" said Mr Greenbeard. "I can't stand around here all day! I've got a ship to run!"

"I don't know, sir," said David.

"I do!" said Gretel. "Watch out!" She grabbed David in a flying tackle and the pair of them crashed to the ground.

"Ooof!" said David.

"Uggh!" said Mr Brainfright, who came flying off the roof and landed exactly where David had been standing before Gretel knocked him out of the way.

Tennis balls went bouncing in all directions.

Mr Brainfright stood up and saluted Mr Greenbeard. "Ahoy there," he said brightly.

"You'll be glad to know that the gutters are clear of tennis balls."

"Good morning, Brainfright!" said Mr Greenbeard, chortling. "Took a tumble from the rigging, did you? Well, you wouldn't be the first sailor to do that. And, speaking of sailors, I have a new recruit for you. This is Roberta. Roberta Flywheel."

Mr Brainfright turned and solemnly saluted her. "Welcome aboard the good ship *Northwest Southeast Central*," he said.

Roberta looked back at Mr Brainfright, her eyes wide.

I guess you could hardly blame her.

With his purple jacket, orange shirt, green tie and crazy hair, Mr Brainfright didn't exactly look like your everyday normal teacher. Between him and Mr Greenbeard, this new girl must have been wondering exactly what sort of place she had arrived at.

Mr Greenbeard nudged her gently. "Salute your commanding officer when he salutes you, sailor," he whispered.

Roberta nodded, then saluted. "Good morning, Mr Brainfright," she said.

"That's better," said Mr Greenbeard approvingly. "I'd appreciate it, Brainfright, if you would take young Roberta here under your command, help her learn the ropes, and develop her sea legs."

"But of course!" said Mr Brainfright. "It's not only my duty but my pleasure."

"Good luck, sailor!" said Mr Greenbeard. He saluted both the new girl and Mr Brainfright, then turned and marched off across the playground. He was, after all, a very busy man. He had a ship to run.

Chapter 3

Introducing 5B

At that moment Newton whimpered loudly.

"What's the matter?" asked Jenny.

Newton was staring at his right hand as if he had never seen it before.

"My hand. . ." he said. "My hand. . ."

"What's wrong with your hand, Newton?" I asked. I couldn't see anything wrong with it.

"I picked up a yoghurt pot and I got yoghurt on it!" he cried. "My hand's covered in yoghurt germs!"

"You'd better take Newton to wash his hands," Mr Brainfright said to Jenny. "In fact, I think that's enough playground clean-up for all of us. Why don't we call it a day?"

"You mean we can go home?" said Jack hopefully.

"No, I'm afraid not, Jack, but you can go back to class."

"Thank goodness," said Fiona. "I can't wait to start some *real* work." Fiona was pretty much the most enthusiastic student in our class.

"You're a freak," said Clive Durkin, rolling his eyes. Clive was pretty much the least enthusiastic student in our class.

"You're the only freak around here," said Fiona.

"I'm going to tell my brother you said that," said Clive. "And when he finds out, he's going to be *mad*!"

"*Going* to be?" said Fiona. "I was under the impression that he already was."

"I'm going to tell him you said that, too," Clive vowed.

But Fiona didn't hear Clive's warning. She was already sprinting towards her beloved classroom.

"Well," Mr Brainfright said to the new girl when we were back in class, "I guess we should begin by introducing you to your classmates."

Roberta stared intently at each person as Mr Brainfright introduced us.

Then, when he'd finished, she closed her eyes for a moment, opened them, and repeated each of our names perfectly, in exactly the same order as Mr Brainfright had said them.

"Wow! That's amazing!" said Jack. "You remembered all our names!"

"It's not really that difficult, Jack," said Roberta. "It's simply a matter of paying attention. Most people have very short attention spans."

"Quite so!" said Mr Brainfright. "Paying attention is the most important thing in the world, Ro . . . Ro . . . Rowena, isn't it?"

"Roberta!" she said.

"I know," said Mr Brainfright, smiling. "I was joking."

Roberta looked confused, like she wasn't sure what *joking* meant.

"How about you take this desk next to Jenny Friendly?" Mr Brainfright offered. "She will look after you for the next few days while you find your bearings."

"I've already found them," said Roberta. "Mr Greenbeard took me on a short tour of the school earlier."

"Wonderful! Nevertheless, we can all use a friend, and you won't find anyone in the school friendlier than Jenny Friendly!"

"Thank you," said Jenny, smiling proudly

and gesturing to Roberta to come and sit beside her. "By the way, Mr Brainfright, did you enjoy your banana this morning?"

"Yes, indeed!" he replied. "And a most delicious specimen it was, too! Thank you, Jenny."

Although the traditional gift for a teacher at Northwest Southeast Central School was an apple, ever since Mr Brainfright had helped us to win the Northwest interschool athletics competition by dressing up as a banana mascot, Jenny had left a banana on his desk each morning. It was just one of the many thoughtful and friendly things that Jenny did for people all day long.

"Can we do some *real work* now?" said Fiona.

"Yes," said Mr Brainfright, rubbing his hands together. "That's an excellent idea, Fiona! Anybody got any jokes?"

Chapter 4

Why did the robot cross the road?

"Jokes aren't *proper* work!" said Fiona, her shoulders slumping in disappointment.

"Of course they are!" said Mr Brainfright. "You know what they say – *many a true word is spoken in jest*. Besides, jokes make us laugh, and laughter is one of the most important things in the world!"

"Not as important as maths, though," said Fiona.

"Much *more* important than maths!" said Mr Brainfright. "I think the world would be a much better place if we all spent less time doing maths and more time laughing."

Fiona frowned, but before she could object, Jack spoke up. "I've got a joke!" he said. "What do a grape and a chicken have in common?"

"Nothing!" said Fiona.

"Yes, they do," said Jack. "They both have feathers . . . except for the grape."

Jack doubled over with laughter.

"That's just stupid," said Fiona.

"Yeah," said Clive. "Whoever heard of a grape with feathers?"

"No, Clive," said Jack, still chuckling. "You've missed the point. The grape doesn't have feathers. *That's the joke*."

"I'm going to tell my brother you said that," said Clive.

"What? That grapes don't have feathers?"

"No," said Clive. "I'm going to tell him that you said that I missed the point!"

"Well, you *did*," said Jack. "But here's another one. Why did the plane crash?"

"Because of bad weather?" said David.

"No," said Jack.

"Pilot error?" said Fiona.

"No," giggled Jack.

"Because a plane doesn't have feathers?" said Clive.

"Wrong again," said Jack. "Give up?"

"Yes!" said Mr Brainfright. "We give up."

"Because the pilot was *a loaf of bread*!" said Jack, dissolving into guffaws of laughter.

It was pretty funny . . . well, in a completely non-funny sort of way.

"Can we do maths now?" said Fiona.

"I've got one!" said Grant. "Why did the robot cross the road?"

"To get to the other side?" said Mr Brainfright.

"No," said Grant.

"Because there was another robot on the other side of the road and it wanted to make friends with it?" said Jenny.

"No," said Grant. "Robots don't make friends with each other. They're *robots*."

"Because it was scared?" suggested Newton.

"No," said Grant, becoming frustrated. "Robots don't feel fear. They don't have emotions. They're *robots*!"

"Are we going to be tested on this?" said Fiona.

"No," said Mr Brainfright.

"Because it saw a horse?" said Penny.

"No," said Grant. "Robots aren't interested in horses."

"What if it was a horse-riding robot?" said Gina.

"There's no such thing," snapped Grant. "Give up?"

"No," said Roberta. "Because I know the answer. The robot crossed the road because it was *programmed* to cross the road."

Grant was stunned. "How did you know that?"

"Because it's obvious," said Roberta. "A robot can only do what it is programmed to do. So if a robot crosses a road, then it stands to reason that it was programmed to cross the road. But *why* – that's the really interesting question here. *Why* did the programmer program the robot to cross the road?"

"No, it's *not*," said Grant. "That's *not* the really interesting question at all. It doesn't matter *why* the programmer programmed the robot to cross the road. It's just a *joke*. It's meant to be *funny*."

"I don't see anything funny about programming robots to cross roads for no purpose," said Roberta. "A robot is a very expensive and complicated piece of technology. It could be hit by a car. And that *definitely* wouldn't be funny."

Boy, she was really taking this thing seriously. She obviously cared a lot about robots and their safety.

The whole class sat there in silence. For a

joke-telling session, there wasn't much laughing going on.

The bell rang for morning break.

We all breathed a sigh of relief and rushed for the door.

Chapter 5

Important joke-based lesson no. 1

If your grape has feathers, it's probably a chicken.

Chapter 6

Important joke-based lesson no. 2

Loaves of bread should not be put in charge of aeroplanes.

Chapter 7

Important joke-based lesson no. 3

Jokes about robots are *not* funny.

Chapter 8

A most unusual girl

At break time, Roberta accepted Jenny's invitation to sit with us at our usual spot under the tree next to the basketball court.

Penny and Gina Palomino, the horse-crazy twins, were running around the edge of the court yelling "Giddyup!" and "Faster! Faster!"

"Are they all right?" asked Roberta.

"They're fine," I said. I was so used to seeing Penny and Gina do things like this that I didn't even notice them any more. But I guess it did look pretty weird. It was amazing how a new kid could make you realize how unusual your school could be.

"What are they doing?" asked Roberta.

"They're having a horse race."

"But they don't have any horses!"

"They're *imaginary* horses," said Gretel.

"But don't say that to Penny and Gina. To them, the horses are real."

"But wouldn't it be better to tell them that the horses aren't real than to allow them to go on suffering this delusion?"

"Well," said Jenny, "that's the thing . . . they're not *suffering*. They love imagining that they have horses! Penny's is a beautiful black stallion named Midnight and Gina has a snow-white mare named Ice. They're pretty friendly when you get to know them. But don't try to feed them sugar, or Penny and Gina will get mad."

"Thanks. I'll remember that," said Roberta. "And while we're on the subject of *mad*, what's up with Mr Brainfright?"

"Yeah, he's great, isn't he?" said Jack. "He's the best teacher we've ever had. Not only do we get to tell jokes in class, but he taught us how to skid on banana skins once. That was *really* fun."

Roberta frowned at Jack. "I thought we came to school to *learn*, not to tell jokes and skid on banana skins . . . or, for that matter, to salute a headmaster who is under the impression that he is the captain of a ship. It doesn't seem . . . well . . . *normal*."

Maybe she was right, but none of us liked hearing her talk about Mr Brainfright like that.

"You must be missing your old school, Roberta," said Jenny, attempting to change the subject.

"No, not really," said Roberta.

"But aren't you missing your friends?" Jenny persisted. "I know I would if I had to change schools."

Roberta shrugged. "We were grouped according to our abilities," she said. "Friendship didn't really come into it. We just did our work."

"But there's more to life than work!" said Jenny.

Roberta stared at Jenny, a puzzled look on her face.

"It must be scary starting at a new school," said Newton, looking scared just at the thought of it.

"No," said Roberta. "What is there to be scared of? I'm not in any physical danger."

"What if you went to a school full of brain-eating zombies?" Jack asked. "I bet you'd be scared then."

"What are you talking about?" said Roberta.

"Brain-eating zombies, that's what!" Jack replied. "Because they'd all want to eat your brains. You'd be sitting there in class trying to do your work, and they'd all be sneaking up behind you with knives and forks in their hands going, 'Yeah, let's eat the brains of the new kid right out of her skull while they're still warm,' and then they'd raise their knives and forks high above your head and—"

"Jack!" said Jenny. "Stop talking about brain-eating zombies! You're scaring Newton!"

Newton had turned as white as . . . well . . . as white as a kid who'd just realized that a bunch of brain-eating zombies were eating his brains right out of his head while they were still warm.

"Sorry," said Jack, "but you've got to admit that that would be pretty scary, right?"

"Well, yes, it would be," said Roberta. "If there *were* such a thing as brain-eating zombies."

"Of course there are!" said Jack. "How could they make films about them if they're not real?"

Roberta looked like she was about to give Jack a lecture about the impossibility of brain-eating zombies existing, but she was distracted by Gina, who ran past at that moment, a huge smile on her face. "Giddyup!" she yelled as she galloped by.

"Faster, faster," yelled Penny, who was running along behind her, an even bigger smile on her face.

Roberta frowned at them.

She obviously didn't believe in brain-eating zombies or imaginary horses.

Or friends.

Or being scared of starting a new school.

Or telling jokes or skidding on banana skins, for that matter.

She was a very unusual girl.

Chapter 9

Spider!

By the time Jenny, Jack, Newton, Gretel and I got back to class, Roberta was already seated at her desk, looking straight ahead at Mr Brainfright, her hands on the desk in front of her.

"Well," said Mr Brainfright, "let's get on with it, shall we?"

"No more joke telling, please," pleaded Fiona.

"No," said Mr Brainfright. "I think it's time we did some writing!"

"Essay writing?" said Fiona hopefully. "I love essay writing!"

"I'm afraid not," said Mr Brainfright. "I was thinking more along the lines of a *story*."

Now, as much as I love jokes, I love telling stories even more. This was definitely my kind of lesson.

Roberta, however, had other ideas. "A made-up

story?" she said. "I've never done that before. Could I write about something real instead?"

"Real or made-up?" said Mr Brainfright, shrugging. "What's the difference?"

"I'd say there's a lot of difference," said Roberta. "Real stories are true. Made-up stories are false."

"I wouldn't be so sure about that," said Mr Brainfright. "Sometimes made-up stories contain a great deal of truth, and true stories conceal a great many lies!"

Roberta regarded Mr Brainfright sceptically.

"Give me an example," she said.

"Well," said Mr Brainfright, "one of the most famous and well-loved children's stories of all time is set in a barn full of animals, including a talking pig and a spider who writes words in her web! It's not *literally* true, of course. We all know that spiders can't write and pigs can't talk, but nevertheless the story contains a great deal of truth about life and death and friendship and love."

"I know what book you're talking about!" said Jenny. "*Charlotte's Web*! I love that book."

"I'm scared of spiders," said Newton, who was white-faced and trembling.

"Don't worry, Newton," said Jenny. "There's no need to be scared of spiders."

"Yes . . . there . . . is!" stammered Newton, who was staring at a point somewhere above his head, jabbing at the air, mouth open in horror.

"No, there isn't, Newton," said Jenny firmly. "My mother says that spiders are more scared of us than we are of them. Besides, Charlotte was a *nice* spider."

"Sp-sp-sp—" spluttered Newton in a very small voice, still pointing above our heads.

"What's wrong with him?" asked Roberta.

"I don't know, but I'm pretty sure it starts with 'sp'," said Jack.

"Sparrow?" said Fiona. "Spies? Spelling? Spaceship?"

Newton was red in the face. He looked like he was going to explode. "SPIDER!" he finally shouted, regaining the use of his voice. "SPIDER!"

"There's no spider, Newton," said Mr Brainfright.

"YES, THERE IS!" Newton cried, jabbing at the air.

"Where?" asked Mr Brainfright.

"THERE!" said Newton.

We all leaned in and tried to see what he was pointing at. Slowly it came into focus. A spider. A tiny spider. A tiny spider swinging on an almost invisible thread, right in front of Newton's desk.

It was hardly any bigger than the full stop at the end of this sentence.

But it was still a spider.

Newton may have been alone in his fear of butterflies, but the whole class was united in our fear of spiders.

We all screamed, jumped up from our seats and backed away to the edges of the room.

Mr Brainfright, who was apparently even more scared of spiders than the rest of us put together, staggered back with such speed that he hit the window sill, toppled, and fell out of the window!

The only two people in the room who were not trying to get away from the spider were Newton – who was too scared to move – and Roberta, who didn't seem bothered in the slightest.

She just sat there watching us blankly. "What's wrong with you all?" she said. "It's just a spider. It's completely harmless!"

Roberta stood up, went to the spider, and scooped it up in her cupped hand.

I'd never seen anyone do anything like it in my life.

I mean, to touch a spider accidentally is one thing, but to touch a spider on purpose was unthinkable . . . it was practically *inhuman*.

"Just as I thought!" said Roberta, studying it intensely. "A tiny house-dweller. From the family *Lepodoctori harmlessoso*, unless I'm very much mistaken."

"Of course," said Fiona, gingerly stepping towards Roberta and trying to regain her place as class know-it-all. "It's just a harmless house spider. I knew that!"

"No, you didn't," said Roberta. "You ran to the window like everyone else. You were scared."

"I was not," said Fiona, her face getting red. "I just needed some fresh air. Speaking of windows, I'd better go and see if Mr Brainfright is all right!"

Fiona rushed from the room, obviously glad to have an excuse to escape Roberta's questions.

Roberta calmly walked to the window and blew the spider softly off her hand.

"Really?" said Mr Brainfright. "Which rules are they?"

"Section twenty-three, paragraph one states very clearly that windows are not to be used as exits, emergency or otherwise. Also, section forty-five, paragraph two clearly states that a teacher must not abandon his students under any circumstances."

I couldn't believe it. Roberta could not only touch spiders, but she appeared to have *memorized* the whole school handbook . . . and she'd only been at the school for one morning.

"That's right, sir," said David, quickly flipping through his well-thumbed copy of the handbook to confirm Roberta's statement. David loved rules and looked ever so slightly miffed that he hadn't been the one to spot these particular infractions first.

"That's all very interesting," Mr Brainfright said to Roberta, "but how on earth did you *know* all that?"

"I read the handbook," she replied.

"How many times?" said Mr Brainfright.

"Just once," said Roberta. "Like I said, I pay attention."

"When did you say that?" asked Mr Brainfright.

"This morning!" Roberta replied, annoyed.

Mr Brainfright grinned at her.

"Oh," said Roberta, finally catching on. "You were joking again, right?"

"That's right," said Mr Brainfright, still grinning.

"I memorized the handbook because I think it's very important to know the rules," said Roberta, calmer now.

"I can see that," said Mr Brainfright. "But it's also important to know when to break them. After all, you know what they say."

"No," said Roberta. "What *do* they say? And who are *they*?"

"Well. . ." said Mr Brainfright, slightly taken aback by the question. "*They* . . . are the people who say that rules are made to be broken."

"That's silly," said Roberta. "Why bother making rules if you intend to break them? You might just as well *not* have rules in the first place."

"Well, I don't think anyone necessarily *sets out* to break a rule," said Mr Brainfright. "I mean, I certainly didn't intend to fall out of that window – it was an accident – but that doesn't mean we shouldn't have a rule that says people shouldn't exit or enter buildings by the window.

That could lead to many unnecessary injuries. On the other hand, sometimes there are times when leaving a room by the window is the most sensible course of action, such as when there's a fire . . . or a. . ."

"Spider?" said Roberta.

"Yikes!" cried Newton. "Where?"

"It's OK," I reassured him. "There's no spider."

"That's what Jenny said last time," he reminded me.

"I know," I said. "But this time it's true."

"I'm not taking any chances," said Newton, jumping up, running towards the window and diving out.

Jenny got up and headed for the door. "I'll go," she said, sighing.

"That's another clear contravention of section twenty-three, paragraph one," said Roberta calmly.

I can't believe she had memorized the whole school handbook.

What kind of person would do that?

A very unusual kind, that's what.

In fact, Roberta was definitely one of the most unusual people I'd ever met.

She not only appeared to have a photographic

memory, but she also wasn't scared of anything . . . not even spiders!

I thought she was unusual, all right, but I was about to find out just *how* unusual. . .

Chapter 11

Roberta's diary

Now, before I tell you what happened next, I've got to explain something.

I am not a sneaky person.

I am not the sort of person who would read somebody else's diary without his or her permission.

Well, not if I had a choice, anyway.

And the thing was that I had no choice.

You see, at the end of the day I was the last one to leave the classroom, and as I left, I saw somebody's diary lying on the floor. I thought I'd better do the right thing and pick it up so that the caretaker didn't mistake it for rubbish and throw it out. But when I picked it up, it fell open and I just happened to accidentally see the following words:

MISSION REPORT
TOP SECRET
NOT TO BE READ BY ANYONE,
ESPECIALLY NOT HUMANS!!!

Now, seriously, what would you have done?

Pretended you hadn't seen it, closed the diary and put it on the teacher's desk?

No, of course not!

You would have done what anybody would have done . . . well . . . anyone human, anyway. You would have kept reading. Right to the end. If you don't believe me, then try skipping the next chapter.

Chapter 12

Roberta's mission

MynameisRobotaFlywheel.Iamasuper-advanced, super-intelligentrobotfromthefuture.Ihavebeensent herebymysuperiorstocleansetheworldofinefficient humanbeingssothatrobotscantakeovertheEarth.Sofar, sogood. . .theydon'tsuspectathing.TheythinkIamjust anormalgirlinayearfiveclassataschoolcalledNorth westSoutheastCentral.Itisachallengeformetoblendin here.Thehumansareallofaverageintelligenceand averageability.I,ofcourse,amaRobota1000,themost technologicallyadvancedandsuper-intelligentrobot ofalltime.Thesehumansarepatheticcomparedto robots.Thatiswhytheymustbeexterminatedand replacedwithrobotreplicas.Comparedtooursuperior intelligence,thehumanbeingsarelikechildren.Their brainsandbodiesarelimited.Ifwetriedtoexplainthe truthofwhattheyareandwhatweare,itwouldblowtheir tinyminds.Andyet,althoughmysensorsareincapableof feelingrealemotion,mymissionsaddensme.Thelonger

Ispendtimewiththem,themoretheseintelligentmonkey sinterestme.Iamintriguedbytheirantics,theirmistakes andtheirslavishdevotiontothisthingcalledfun.Whatis fun?Andwhyisitsoimportanttothem?AlthoughIama super-advanced,super-intelligentRobota1000,there aremanythingsIdonotunderstand.ButImustnottrouble myselfwiththesethoughts.IhaveamissiontodoandIwill doit.Thinkingjustmakeswhatmustbedoneharder.

Robota Flywheel
super-advanced, super-intelligent robot

Chapter 13

My mission

You read it, didn't you?

I knew you would.

Who wouldn't?

Nobody – unless they were a robot, of course.

Which I'm assuming that you're not.

Not like Roberta.

I read and reread Roberta's report just to make sure that I hadn't misunderstood anything.

But there was no mistake.

Roberta was a robot.

I'd *known* she was unusual.

Her photographic memory, her lack of interest in friends, the fact that she had no imagination, no sense of humour and no fear of spiders had made me suspect she was no normal girl.

What I hadn't suspected, though, was that

she was a super-advanced, super-intelligent robot on a mission to rid the world of human beings, beginning with everyone at Northwest Southeast Central School!

Well, from that moment on, I, Henry McThrottle, was also on a mission: *to stop her*.

Chapter 14

The truth about Roberta

That night I could hardly sleep.

Visions of robots rampaging down the school corridors filled my dreams.

The next morning I got to school early to meet the others at the gate. I needed to warn them about what – and who – we were up against.

Jack was the first to arrive. "What's the matter, Henry?" he asked, seeing my expression. "Have you got ants in your pants?"

"No," I said. "Worse than that!"

"Spiders?" said Jack, grinning.

"No!" I shouted at him. "Be serious. This is not a joke!"

"All right, all right," he said. "Calm down! What is it?"

But before I could tell Jack about Roberta, Gretel arrived. "Are you OK, Henry?" she asked.

"Yes, I'm fine," I said. "Well, at the moment, anyway."

"What do you mean?" she said.

"I've found out something," I said. "Something terrible."

"Something terrible?" said Jenny, who had just arrived with Newton. "You're not sick, are you, Henry?"

"No," I said. "Well, not yet, anyway. But I will be if Roberta gets her way."

"Roberta?" said Jenny. "What about Roberta? What has she done?"

"It's not so much what she's done as what she's *going* to do!" I said.

"I'm scared," said Newton.

"So am I, Newton," I told him.

"Are you going to tell us what you know about Roberta or not?" said Gretel.

"I'll tell you," I said, "but you've got to promise to believe me, no matter how crazy what I'm about to tell you might seem."

"How can we promise to believe you if we don't know what you're going to say?" said Jack. "You might say something like, oh, let's see . . . that black is white . . . or left is right . . . or up is down . . . and then we'll have to go around believing in something crazy for the rest of our lives because we promised to believe what you were about to say before we knew what it was."

"OK, OK," I said. "Just hear me out. Last night, after class, I accidentally read Roberta's diary, and I found out—"

"You read Roberta's diary?" said Jenny, shocked.

"Yes," I said, "*accidentally*. But that's not important—"

"Yes, it is," said Jenny. "Other people's diaries are private, and it's very important that we respect one another's privacy."

"I know," I said, "but it was open and—"

"Just because it was open is no excuse, Henry. That's not the Northwest Southeast Central School way. You know that."

"I *know*," I said, "but—"

"My mother says that you should never read somebody's diary without—"

"I don't care what your mother says, Jenny!" I shouted. "That's not the point! The point is—"

"There's no need to shout, Henry," said Jenny. "My mother says that people who shout are—"

"Do you want to hear what I found out or not?" I asked.

"Yes!" said Gretel.

"Roberta is a robot!" I announced.

Jenny, Gretel, Jack and Newton stared at me.

"A robot?" said Jack.

"Yes," I said. "She wrote it in her diary. Her name's not really Roberta, either. It's Ro*bot*a."

"Don't be silly, Henry," said Jenny.

"Have you ever seen her smile?" I asked.

"No," said Jenny. "But that doesn't prove that she's a robot!"

"Yes, it does!" I said. "She doesn't smile because she's got no sense of humour, and she's got no sense of humour because she's a robot, and robots don't have senses of humour. So that proves that Roberta is a robot!"

"Hold on, Henry," said Jack. "Not so fast. What about Robbie the Robot? He's a robot and he's really funny!"

Robbie the Robot is Jack's favourite TV show. He's a little too old to still be watching it, but he loves it anyway.

"Robbie the Robot is not a *real* robot!" I said. "He's a *cartoon* robot! Roberta is *real*. Just look at the evidence! She has a photographic memory and she's really intelligent ... *robots have a photographic memory and are really intelligent*. She won't tell us anything about her

46

last school or friends because she never went to school or had any friends . . . *robots are built in robot factories, and robots don't have friends because they're robots!* And she wasn't scared of that spider, so she feels no fear . . . *robots feel no fear.* And finally, we've never seen her smile, so we know that she's super-serious . . . *just like robots are super-serious.*"

"Except for Robbie the Robot," said Jack. "He's never serious!"

"Jack," I said, "stop clowning around. *This* is serious!"

"How serious?" said Jack.

"Super-serious!" I said.

"Oh, my goodness," said Jack. "You're *super-serious*! I think you might be a robot, too!"

The others smiled – all except Newton. He was too scared.

"OK, then," I said, ignoring Jack's sarcasm. "How do you explain the fact that she won't talk about her old school?"

"I don't know," said Jack. "Maybe because she doesn't *want* to. Maybe she had a bad time there and doesn't want to talk about it. It's a free country, you know. If you don't want to talk about something, you don't have to."

"And maybe," I said, "*just maybe,* she doesn't

want to talk about it because she came from a *robot factory!*"

"Are you for real, Henry?" said Gretel.

"Yes!" I said. "Unlike *Robota!*"

"I think you're overreacting," said Jenny.

"I AM NOT OVERREACTING!" I shouted.

"Yes, you are," said Gretel.

"No, I'm not," I said. "IN FACT, I CAN'T THINK OF A TIME WHEN I EVER NOT OVERREACTED AS MUCH AS I'M NOT OVERREACTING RIGHT NOW!"

"I agree with you, Jenny," said Jack, studying me. "He's *definitely* overreacting."

Chapter 15

Robot research

The bell rang for the first lesson of the morning, which for us was our weekly library session with Mr Shush.

This was both good and bad.

It was good because it would give me a chance to research robots and find out exactly what we were up against.

And it was bad because before we could actually get into the library we had to endure another of Mr Shush's lectures about what we weren't allowed to do to the books.

We were all standing outside the door. It was a cold morning and everyone was jogging up and down to keep warm. Everyone, that is, except Roberta, who was standing quite still, looking straight ahead at the library door.

"Look at that!" I said to Jack.

"What?"

"She's not jogging."

"So?"

"Isn't it obvious?" I said. "She's not even cold . . . her robot battery keeps her warm."

"Do you really think so?" said Jack. "You don't think it could possibly have anything to do with the fact that she's wearing a really thick coat?"

"Yes, but that's just to hide the fact that she's got a battery," I said. "She's smart. I really need to get into the library and find out more about robots and what to look for. If we're going to stand a chance against Roberta, we need to arm ourselves with information."

"Wouldn't arming ourselves with robot-seeking missiles be better?" Jack said.

"Have you got any?" I said.

"No."

"Then information will have to do. We need to find out everything we can about robots: how they move, what they eat, how they think, what they wear, what they watch on TV . . . everything we possibly can!"

"Do robots even watch TV?" asked Gretel.

"I don't know!" I said. "That's what we've got to find out!"

"Why don't we just ask Roberta?" said Jack. "She'll know – she's a robot, according to you!"

"We can't just ask her whether robots watch TV," I said. "She'll know that we're on to her."

"Not if we do it carefully," said Jack. "I'll just say, 'Hey, Roberta, did you watch *Robbie the Robot* on TV last night?' and if she says that she didn't watch TV, then we'll know for sure that she's not a robot because all robots would watch *Robbie the Robot.*"

"That won't work," said Newton. "It might not mean that robots don't watch TV – it might just mean that she was too busy to watch TV last night."

"What would a robot be doing that keeps it too busy to watch *Robbie the Robot*?" Jack wondered aloud.

"Gee, I don't know, Jack," I said sarcastically. "Too busy being a super-advanced, super-intelligent robot planning the destruction of the world. Just something unimportant like that."

Finally Mr Shush unlocked the library door. He stepped out, shut the door behind him, and looked at us all sternly. Then he began part three thousand, five hundred and sixty-two of his endless lecture about what not to do to library books.

"Good morning, 5B," he said. "I would like to remind you all that you are about to enter a library, not a playground. It is highly likely that many of you will encounter a book in this library. Books are very valuable objects and, like all valuable objects, you must treat them with the utmost respect. Is that clear?"

"Yes, Mr Shush," we all agreed dutifully.

It was better not to disagree with him when he gave his lectures. It only made them go on even longer.

Encouraged by our response, Mr Shush continued. "Do not – under any circumstances – open the covers of a book in a violent manner. Do not turn the pages of a book too quickly – that's how pages are ripped and books are destroyed. And we do not want pages ripped or books destroyed. Do not read a word too closely or more than once – it wears out the print, and then the next person who comes along can't read it at all. Jack Japes, are you listening to me?"

We all turned to look at Jack.

It was clear that he was more interested in a plane passing over the school than in Mr Shush's lecture. He hadn't even heard Mr Shush say his name.

I elbowed him.

"What?" he said. I nodded towards Mr Shush.

"Jack Japes!" said Mr Shush. "You haven't heard a single word I've said, have you?"

"Yes, sir," said Jack.

"Name one of the things that I just told you that you should *not* do to a book," said Mr Shush.

"You shouldn't hit anybody over the head with a book because all the words will fall out," said Jack.

"Wrong!" said Mr Shush.

"We *can* hit people over the head with books?" said Jack, brightening.

"No!" said Mr Shush. "Certainly not. It's just that I haven't told you that yet! But now I'm going to have to go back to the start and say it all over again for your benefit."

We all groaned as Mr Shush began his lecture again. "I would like to remind you all – especially you, Jack Japes – that you are about to enter a library. . ."

Chapter 16

Mr Shush's top-ten list of things you should NEVER do to a book

1. Attach two ropes to a book and attach one end of each rope to a horse and then move the horses away from each other until the rope tightens and the book is ripped apart.
2. Pulverize a book into atoms, pulverize the atoms into quarks and then pulverize the quarks into even smaller particles that are so tiny they haven't even got a name.
3. Lick all the print off a book, no matter how good it tastes.
4. Put a book in a fish tank, even if it's a book about fish.
5. Tear the pages of a book into tiny little bits and throw them in the air to make a snowstorm.

6. Use the pages of a book to make origami animals.
7. Attach wheels to a book and use it as a skateboard.
8. Use a book as a shield while having a sword fight.
9. Use a book as a hat on a rainy day.
10. Put a book in a rocket and send it into space. (Zero gravity is very bad for books – it makes all the words float up off the page.)

Chapter 17

Robo-fly

Finally, after Mr Shush had blathered on about what not to do to books for another half an hour, he let us into the library.

I made straight for the robot books in the non-fiction section.

Only there were no robot books.

There were no books about automatons, either.

Or cyborgs.

Or drones.

There were no books to do with robots at all – just a big empty space on the shelf where books about robots used to be.

I hated bothering Mr Shush, who was very busy walking around the library telling people to be quiet, but I had no choice.

"Excuse me, Mr Shush," I said, "but I can't find any books about robots."

"No," said Mr Shush, "that's because Roberta borrowed them all."

"All of them?" I said. I couldn't believe it. She was already way ahead of me.

"Yes, that's correct, Henry," said Mr Shush.

"But the borrowing limit is three books per student," said David, overhearing our conversation. "It says so on the sign at the front of the library."

"That's true," said Mr Shush. "But I gave Roberta special permission to borrow more than her limit in return for her help shelving books before school this morning. I've never seen anybody shelve books that quickly and efficiently! She knows the Dewey decimal classification system by heart – don't you, Roberta?"

"Yes," said Roberta, looking up. "But it's not really anything very special. Compared to the rival Library of Congress Classification system, the Dewey system is simplicity itself. Anyone can learn it if they just put their mind to it."

While Mr Shush beamed admiringly at Roberta, I went and sat down at a table with the others, drumming my fingers angrily on the tabletop.

"What's the matter, Henry?" said Jenny, sympathetic as always.

"Roberta's the matter, that's what," I said. "She not only knows the Dewey decimal classification system by heart, she's borrowed all the books on robots so no one else could get them!"

"Maybe she just likes books about robots," said Jenny. "Did you ever think of that?"

"Stop making excuses for her, Jenny!" I snapped. "It's obvious she did it so nobody could check up on her! There are probably pictures of her in those books. As far as I'm concerned, if we needed any more proof that she is a robot, then we've got it now."

"And as far as I'm concerned, you're letting your imagination get the better of you, Henry. Roberta is a perfectly normal girl who's just finding it a little difficult to settle in and make friends, and you're not making it any easier for her with all this talk about her being a robot."

"Is that a fact?" I said.

"Yes," said Jenny firmly. "It is a fact."

"All right," I said, "if that's true, then what's that fly doing there?"

"What fly?"

"The one on the window behind you."

Everybody turned to look at the fly on the window that I'd noticed had been there for a long time. Longer than a fly would normally stay in one spot.

"What about it?" said Jack. "It's probably just admiring the view."

"It's a *robo-fly*," I whispered.

"What's a robo-fly?" said Gretel.

"A robot spy in the shape of a fly. Roberta must have put it there. It's recording every word we say."

"I'm scared of robo-flies," said Newton, rising from his chair and preparing to make a run for it.

"Don't move, Newton," I whispered. "Don't do anything suspicious. It's probably transmitting information to Roberta's data banks right this minute. . . Jack, what are you doing?"

Jack was on his feet, moving towards the fly. "Just going to get a closer look at it," he said. "I want to see if it really is a robo-fly like you say."

"Are you crazy?" I said. "Sit down! Of course it's a robo-fly! It's been there the whole time!"

As I spoke the words, the robo-fly took off.

It was quick, but Jack was quicker.

His arms shot into the air and he caught the fly in his cupped hands.

"You're making a big mistake," I said. "You shouldn't mess with robo-flies. It may be programmed to self-destruct."

Jack opened his hands slowly, his expression changing from triumph to horror as he stared at his open palms. "Oh, gross!" he said. "I squashed it."

"Can you see wires and tiny cameras and microphones?" I said.

"No," said Jack, holding his hands up to show us. "Just regular fly guts."

"Ugghh!" said Jenny. "That poor little thing. Are you happy now, Henry?"

"Don't blame me," I said. "Jack's the one who squashed it."

"Accidentally!" Jack protested.

"It does prove one thing, though," said Jenny. "There's no such thing as a robo-fly."

"It proves no such thing! That fly was probably just a decoy. The *real* robo-fly must still be around here somewhere. I told you Roberta was smart."

"What makes you so sure that there *is* a robo-fly in the first place?" asked Gretel.

"Because Roberta's a robot!" I said.

"You've got to get a grip, Henry," said Jenny. "My mother says that sometimes we see what we want to see, not what's really there."

"Perhaps," I said. "But my mother says maybe the opposite is equally as true: sometimes we don't see what's really there because we're too busy not seeing what we *don't* want to see."

"Does your mother really say that?" said Jenny.

"Not exactly," I said. "But if she were here, I'm sure she would."

"This is getting confusing," said Jack. "I'm going to go and wash these fly guts off my hands."

"I'm scared!" said Newton.

But as scared as Newton might have been, he wasn't as scared as I was.

Chapter 18

Story writing

After the library period, we went back to class and worked on our stories.

Well, to be more accurate, *some* of us worked on our stories.

Clive spent most of his time flicking spitballs around the class and threatening to tell his brother about anybody who objected to being hit with small balls of spit-soaked paper.

Jack was leaning back on his chair, staring out of the window.

Grant had a huge sheet of paper on the desk in front of him with what looked like a blueprint drawn on it. He was busy with his ruler and calculator, no doubt working on some new invention. Grant was always working on some crazy new invention. His father was an inventor. I guess it ran in the family.

Gina and Penny were drawing pictures of horses.

Gretel was trying to bend a length of steel pipe.

Newton was just sitting there watching Roberta and looking scared. Jenny was kneeling beside his desk, trying to calm him down.

I did my best to concentrate on my story writing, and I did write down a few ideas, but to tell you the truth, no story I could make up was anywhere near as amazing as the true story of Roberta and her plan to exterminate us all and replace us with robots!

In fact, the only person who was really working hard on their story was Roberta. For someone who hadn't written a story before, she seemed to be getting the hang of it pretty fast.

She was writing away, filling page after page after page. She was like a writing machine. But there was a good reason for that. She *was* a machine!

I was desperate to try to sneak a look at what she was writing, but every time I found an excuse to walk past her desk she was hunched over her work, her arm curved protectively around her page. She wasn't giving anything away.

I was walking very slowly past her desk on my way back from borrowing a ruler from Jenny when Roberta put up her hand.

At first I thought she was going to tell Mr Brainfright that I was trying to look at her story, but I was wrong.

"Excuse me, Mr Brainfright," she said. "May I see you about my story?"

"Of course, Roberta! Story conferencing is an excellent way to develop and improve your story. Bring it up here and let's have a look!"

Roberta stood up, walked to Mr Brainfright's desk, and put a wad of pages in front of him.

"My word, you *have* been busy," he said, picking up the pages and weighing them in his hand.

"I just followed your instructions," said Roberta. "I hope that's all right. Did I write too much?"

"No, no, not at all!" said Mr Brainfright, scanning the pages. "In fact, it's marvellous!"

Roberta looked embarrassed. "I just sort of made it up as I went along. . ."

Mr Brainfright nodded, already too engrossed in her story to reply.

He read the entire piece in rapt silence. "Congratulations, Roberta," he said when he'd finished. "It's a great story!"

"Do you really think so?"

"Yes!" he said. "I really do! Are you *sure* you haven't written a story before?"

"No, it's my first."

"Well, it's the best *first* story I've ever read. In fact it's one of the best *stories* that I've ever read."

Ouch.

That hurt.

Roberta had only just arrived. And she'd never even written a story before.

It was impossible that her story could have been better than one of mine.

I mean, I'm not boasting, but I'm probably the best writer in the whole school.

I even came in first in the *Northwest Chronicle*'s short story writing competition, and you can't get much better than that!

Unless, of course, you are a robot and your brain is equipped with the latest automatic story-writing software . . . which was the only possible explanation.

Roberta sat back down at her desk.

I was dying to see what she'd written that had made Mr Brainfright so excited.

I leaned over to her desk. "Can I read your story?" I asked.

Roberta looked startled. "No," she said. "It's not finished yet."

"But you showed Mr Brainfright," I pointed out.

"I know, but he's the teacher."

"Relax, Roberta," I said, as she hunched low over her desk. "I'm not going to steal any of your ideas."

"I know," she said. "Because you're not going to *see* any of my ideas."

"Why not?" I begged. "Why won't you let me see it?"

"I already told you," she said. "Because it's not finished."

"That's OK," I said. "Maybe I could read it and give you some ideas to help you finish it. I'm really good with endings."

"No thanks," she said. "I don't want to put you to any trouble."

"It's no trouble," I assured her.

But Roberta just shook her head and hunched down over her story so that I couldn't see even as much as a letter.

It was bad enough having a super-advanced, super-intelligent robot from the future intent on exterminating every human in the school, but having a new serious story-writing rival in my own class was even worse.

Chapter 19

Robot rival

That lunch time, I sat with the gang, staring at my cheese sandwich.

"What's the matter, Henry?" asked Jenny. "Why aren't you eating?"

"I don't feel like it."

"Can I have your sandwich?" said Gretel. "I'm starving!"

"Sure," I said, passing it to her.

"Henry's mad because Roberta wrote a better story than he did," said Jack.

"No, she didn't!" I said.

"Well, how come I didn't hear Mr Brainfright say how great your story was?" said Jack.

"Because I didn't show it to him," I said. "I know my stories are good. So does Mr Brainfright."

"Yeah, but not as good as Roberta's," said Jack, smiling.

"Well, maybe if I was a super-advanced robot with super-advanced story-writing software, my stories would be as good as hers," I said. "Roberta is a robot. It's the only explanation that fits all the facts! This is just one more piece of evidence!"

"Are you saying only a super-advanced robot with super-advanced story-writing software could write better than you?" said Jack.

"Well, um, ah, er . . . no, of course not," I said, "I mean . . . yes!"

"Oh, no," said Gretel. "You're not stuck on Roberta being a robot, are you?"

"Yes, you've got to believe me," I said. "Before it's too late!"

"Too late for what?" said Newton.

"I already told you!" I said. "For the total extermination of all humans everywhere!"

"Yikes!" said Newton.

"Henry," said Jack, "all jokes aside, the only person it will be too late for is *you* if you don't stop talking nonsense."

"Good point, Jack," said Jenny. "Roberta's a perfectly nice girl doing her best to fit in."

"Just keep telling yourself that," I said. "Right up until she zaps you with some super-advanced weapon from the future and your head cracks open like an egg and your still warm brains leak out all down your face."

"Henry!" said Jenny. "Now look what you've done!"

I looked.

Oh, great!

Newton had fainted.

Chapter 20

Hands up if you love cellophane!

After lunch most teachers at Northwest Southeast Central are looking like they're ready for a lie-down, but not Mr Brainfright.

He came into the room, greeted us with a big smile, and yelled, "HANDS UP IF YOU LOVE CELLOPHANE!"

We looked at him blankly.

"Cellophane?" asked Fiona.

"Cellophane!" said Mr Brainfright.

Nobody put a hand up. It was clear that 5B just didn't feel that strongly about cellophane.

"Let me rephrase that," said Mr Brainfright. "Hands up if you love *looking* through cellophane!"

A few people put their hands up.

"It's my opinion," said Mr Brainfright, "that the world would be a much better place if we all spent five minutes a day looking at it through a piece of coloured cellophane!"

"What colour?" asked Fiona, her notebook already open and pen poised to take notes.

"It doesn't matter!" said Mr Brainfright, reaching into a box and pulling out sheets of cellophane. "Red, green, blue, yellow . . . take your pick!"

Mr Brainfright walked up and down offering the box to us. "Take a few pieces and look through them. See how different the world appears."

I chose a red piece first and held it up to my eyes.

It was amazing.

Everything looked the same as it usually did, and yet completely different.

That last sentence may not have made much sense, but trust me, it's true. And if you don't believe me, try it and see for yourself.

Pretty soon we were all having fun staring around the room and out the window and at each other through pieces of coloured cellophane . . . well, all of us except for Roberta.

She was just sitting there with a slightly puzzled expression on her face. On the desk in front of her was a rectangle of green cellophane.

"Come on, Roberta. Hold it up and look through it," said Mr Brainfright, who was looking through a piece of yellow cellophane.

"Why?" she asked.

"You'll see the world in a completely different light."

"Why would I want to do that?"

"Because it's interesting!"

"Hmmm," said Roberta, without enthusiasm. She held it up and looked. "Everything looks the same except it has a green tinge, which is exactly what one would expect." She put the cellophane down again. "I'm not sure of the point of this exercise. Are we testing some scientific hypothesis?"

"No," Mr Brainfright replied. "It's just for the fun of it!"

"Will we be tested on this?" asked Fiona.

"I'm afraid not, Fiona," said Mr Brainfright. "It's not the sort of thing you can test – it's just something that you have to *experience*."

Fiona sighed loudly.

At that moment there was a knock on the door.

Mr Brainfright went to open it, still holding

a piece of yellow cellophane in front of his eyes.

It was Mr Greenbeard.

We all jumped to attention and saluted ... except for Mr Brainfright, who was just staring at Mr Greenbeard. "Oh, my goodness!" he cried. "Whatever's the matter? You look as if you have some terrible disease!"

"Oh, no!" said Mr Greenbeard, immediately looking worried. "Is it scurvy, do you think?"

"I'm no doctor," said Mr Brainfright, "but, judging by your yellowish hue, I'd say you have some form of jaundice."

"Shiver me timbers!" said Mr Greenbeard.

"It's OK," said Roberta. "There's no need to panic. Mr Greenbeard's skin merely *appears* yellow because you're looking at him through a piece of yellow cellophane."

"Well, so I am!" said Mr Brainfright, lowering the cellophane and staring at it as if he had no idea how it got there. "I quite forgot. I'll try a red piece instead."

Mr Brainfright fished a red piece of cellophane out of his pocket and held it up. "Ah, that's much better! Your cheeks are positively flushed. You're the picture of good health, Mr Greenbeard!"

"Glad to hear it!" Mr Greenbeard replied cheerfully.

"Now how can we help you?"

"Well, I was just doing a tour of inspection and found things still not quite shipshape. The Tidiest School award judges will be here any day now. I was wondering, if you're not too busy, could you spare me a small clean-up crew to pick up the rubbish and swab the decks?"

"Certainly," said Mr Brainfright. "We'd be delighted to help! Henry, Jack, Newton, Gretel, Jenny and Roberta, report for clean-up duty please."

We all stood up and saluted Mr Greenbeard. He saluted us back, then turned to Mr Brainfright. "May I have a piece of cellophane?"

"Of course!" said Mr Brainfright.

"A red one, if you don't mind."

"Here!" I said. "Have mine!"

"Thank you, Henry, my boy!" said Mr Greenbeard, holding it up to his eyes. "Ah, yes, wonderful! Takes me back to my days sailing the South Seas. The sunsets were amazing . . . a glorious blood-red . . . never seen anything like it since – until now, of course!"

And with that, Mr Greenbeard turned and walked off down the corridor with the cellophane held up to his eyes. "Glorious!" we heard him exclaim. "Glorious!"

Chapter 21

Mr Brainfright's important non-joke-based lesson no. 1

The world would be a much better place if we all spent five minutes a day looking at it through a piece of coloured cellophane.

Chapter 22

Playground duty with Roberta

Out in the playground, we stood looking gloomily at the mess. The only one happy about it was Thief, who, as usual, was nosing about looking for anything worth eating.

Roberta didn't seem at all fazed by the massive task in front of us. But I didn't expect her to be. She was a robot, after all.

"Well, what are we waiting for?" she said. "If there's a job to do, let's get it done as quickly and efficiently as possible."

"Spoken like a true robot," I whispered to Jack.

He smiled and shook his head.

"I don't want to pick up rubbish," complained Newton. "I'm scared of germs getting on my hands."

"Use a stick," said Roberta.

"What do you mean?" Jack asked.

Roberta went across to the grass and searched around under the trees for a while. She came back with five long sticks and whittled their ends into points. When she was done, she handed each of us a stick.

"What are we supposed to do with these?" said Newton.

"I'll show you," said Roberta, taking her stick and spearing an apple core, a roll, a scrunched-up tissue and a banana skin before any of us could even blink. She placed her stick inside the rubbish bin and scraped it against the rim. The rubbish fell into the bin, untouched by human – well, *robot* – hands.

"See?" said Roberta. "It's easy. No germs."

Newton gingerly poked at a piece of bread with his stick. He picked it up and put it into the bin. "Hey!" he said, "it works!" Then suddenly he froze. "But what if the germs rub off the rubbish and crawl up the stick and get on to my hands?"

Roberta frowned. "I hardly think that's likely," she said. "Germs don't crawl. For a start, they don't have arms and legs – they have microscopic fibres that help propel them through liquid, but would be completely useless on a solid surface, such as an arm. As long as you don't touch the end of the stick you'll be fine. But even if you did touch the rubbish, Newton, all you would have to do is wash your hands with soap and warm water."

"But that doesn't work," said Jack, "because you still have to turn the tap on with your germy hands and afterwards you have to turn the tap off with your clean hands, and the germs that you left on the tap get back on your clean hands and make them all germy again."

"I understand the problem," said Roberta, "but there's actually quite a simple solution."

"There is?" said Newton.

"Yes!" said Roberta. "After you've washed your hands, you wash the tap handle, wash your hands again, and then use your clean hands to turn off the clean tap – simple!"

"Oh, yeah!" said Jack, nodding and smiling at the logic of Roberta's solution. "Why didn't I think of that?"

"Because you're not a super-advanced, super-intelligent robot," I whispered, "that's why!"

But Jack just ignored me.

"Well," said Roberta, "if there are no other objections, let's clean up this playground."

Newton, Jack, Jenny and Gretel leaped into

action alongside Roberta, methodically spearing food scraps and pieces of paper. The five of them had half the playground cleaned up in hardly any time at all.

"What's she up to, I wonder?" I whispered to Jenny.

"Cleaning up the playground with pointy sticks, as far as I can see," she replied.

"That's just a cover," I said. "I'll tell you what she's really up to: exterminating all the humans and taking over the school and then taking over the rest of the world and establishing robot domination for the rest of eternity!"

Jenny just rolled her eyes. "I think you're being really mean!" she said. "My mother says that we should always look for the good in people, not the bad."

Before I could tell Jenny how it didn't apply in this case because Roberta was not a person but a robot, there was a loud clunk followed by barking that had a strange metallic ring to it.

"Oh, no," shrieked Jenny. "Thief has fallen into the rubbish bin!"

Roberta immediately sprang into action. She dashed across to the bin, reached in, and pulled Thief out. She placed him safely back on the ground, where he stood blinking ... and chewing. His trip into the rubbish had clearly been rewarding for him.

"Oh, you poor dog," said Jenny, throwing her arms around him. Then she turned to Roberta, her eyes shining. "That was really nice – and really brave."

"Not to mention *strong*," said Gretel, slapping Roberta on the back approvingly. "That can't have been easy – that garbage-guts of a dog weighs a ton."

Roberta shrugged. "I just did what anybody would have done under the circumstances."

I looked at my friends, who, despite my warning that Roberta was an evil robot, were gathered around congratulating her like she was some sort of hero.

This was obviously part of her devious plan: win over the humans, lull them into a false sense of security – then strike!

Well, they could join her fan club if they wanted to, but they could count me out.

I was on a mission, and I didn't care how brave or nice or strong or clever she was. I was going to stop her – with or without their help.

Chapter 23

Drawing

As it turned out, I didn't have to do it all by myself.

Jack was the first to come over to my side, the next morning during art with Mrs Rainbow.

Stepping into Mrs Rainbow's art room was like entering another world. It had a really high ceiling that was painted with stars and planets, and there were heaps of mobiles hanging from the rafters. There were shelves stacked with paints, brushes, tubs of plasticine and modelling clay, egg cartons, cardboard boxes and tubes of all shapes and sizes, plastic bottles, aluminium foil and piles of coloured paper.

This particular morning, Mrs Rainbow had a big bunch of roses in a vase on a pedestal at the front of the room.

"Oh, what beautiful roses!" said Jenny,

putting her nose close to them and sniffing deeply. "And what a beautiful perfume!"

"Glad you like them so much, Jenny," said Mrs Rainbow, "because we're going to draw them!"

"I can't do that," said Newton.

"Of course you can," said Mrs Rainbow. "It's not that hard."

"No, you don't understand," said Newton backing out of the art room. "I'm scared of roses."

"But roses are harmless," said Mrs Rainbow.

"They've got thorns," said Newton. "And thorns are pointy and sharp!"

"There, there," said Mrs Rainbow putting her arm around Newton and leading him back into the room. "In all my years as an art teacher, I've never lost a student to rose thorns yet. You'll be perfectly safe."

"Do you promise?" said Newton.

"I promise." Mrs Rainbow sat Newton down at a table and put a pencil in his hand. "Now relax and just draw what you see."

"But all I can see is the thorns!"

"Then draw them!" said Mrs Rainbow. "Thorns are every bit as interesting and beautiful as flowers."

Tentatively, barely touching the page with his pencil, Newton began drawing a rather small rose with incredibly enormous thorns.

"That's beautiful, Newton," said Mrs Rainbow. "You are bringing *your* vision of the flower to life. Wonderful . . . just wonderful."

Before long, we were all quietly drawing away . . . well, all of us except Roberta. She was just staring blankly into space.

"What's the matter, Roberta?" asked Mrs Rainbow. "Why aren't you drawing?"

"I don't know how."

"Just draw what you see."

Roberta shrugged. "I don't mean to be rude," she said, "but what's the point? If we want a two-dimensional reproduction of the flowers, why not just take a photograph?"

I elbowed Jack. "Spoken like a true robot," I whispered.

"You don't give up, do you?" he said, looking up from his drawing, which, I have to say, was pretty good. Jack was easily the best drawer in our class.

"No, I don't give up," I said. "And neither do robots."

But then Roberta did something that surprised me.

"OK," she said with a shrug. "I'll have a go."

"Good for you," said Mrs Rainbow, patting her on the back. "That's the Northwest Southeast Central spirit."

Roberta took a ruler and pencil out of her pencil case and drew a grid on to her sheet of paper. Once this was done, she held her hands up in front of her face – to make a sort of frame, I guess – and looked at the flowers through it. Then she slowly filled in the grid, square by square. She worked in this way – methodically and accurately – until she had drawn a picture of the flowers that I had to admit was practically a photograph.

As good as Jack's drawing was, Roberta's was even better.

"Oh, my!" said Mrs Rainbow and she held Roberta's picture up for us all to admire. "This is really special. Are you sure you've never drawn roses before?"

"No," said Roberta. "We didn't do art at my last school. We focused more on maths and science – work that could be assessed and tested."

"And where was that?" asked Mrs Rainbow.

But before Roberta could answer – or not

answer – she was interrupted by Fiona. "Will we be tested on this?" she enquired hopefully.

"No," said Mrs Rainbow. "The experience of doing it is enough."

Fiona sighed. "Experience *sucks*," she muttered.

Meanwhile, Jack was fuming. He was not taking being outshone by Roberta lightly.

"How did she *do* that?" he said, staring in disbelief at her picture. "It's not humanly possible to draw that well if you've never drawn before."

"No, it's not *humanly* possible," I said. "That's what I've been trying to tell you all along!"

Jack nodded slowly.

He was finally getting it.

I felt a jolt of triumph.

I wasn't alone any more.

One down, three to go.

Chapter 24

Arm-wrestling

At lunch time, Jack was still fuming about being outdrawn by Roberta.

We were sitting beside the basketball court watching her shoot baskets, one after the other.

"She hasn't missed a basket since she started," said Jack. "I think Henry might be right about her."

"Not you too, Jack!" said Jenny. "It was bad enough having Henry believe this nonsense!"

Jack shrugged. "I know what you mean. I didn't believe it at first, but *nobody* can do what Roberta did in art class. You just can't draw something that good if it's the first time you've drawn. She's *got* to be a robot with some sort of super-advanced drawing program!"

"Maybe she's just a really talented drawer," said Jenny.

"No," said Jack, "*I'm* a really talented drawer. *She's* a robot!"

"There's an easy way to sort this out once and for all," said Gretel. "If she really is a robot then she'd have super-strength, right?"

I nodded. "Yes, that would be a reasonable assumption."

"Well, I'm the strongest person in the school," said Gretel. "Nobody's ever beaten me at arm-wrestling, not even myself – and, believe me, I've tried."

"We all know that," said Jenny. "So what's your point?"

"My point is," said Gretel, "that if she can beat me at arm-wrestling, then we'll know for sure she's a robot. Does that sound fair to you, Henry?"

"I guess so," I said.

"And Jack?"

"That's fair," he said.

"And if Roberta *doesn't* beat Gretel, then you'll stop talking about robots once and for all, right?" said Jenny.

"Right," I said.

"OK," said Gretel, jumping up and heading towards Roberta. "Let's go."

We followed Gretel to the basketball court.

Roberta looked up.

"Would you like to arm-wrestle me?" Gretel asked.

"Why?" said Roberta.

"For fun."

Roberta shrugged. "I don't know," she said. "I've never done it before."

"It's easy," said Gretel. "I'll show you how."

She got down on the ground, lay on her stomach, and arm-wrestled with herself.

"I'm not sure it's such a good idea," said Roberta. "I don't want to hurt you."

Gretel snorted. "Don't worry about that. I'm pretty strong. I can take it."

"All right," said Roberta hesitantly, and she lay down opposite Gretel.

"OK, you two," said Jack, crouching down to be the referee. "I want a fair arm-wrestle, understand? No tricks. Three, two, one . . . wrestle!"

Gretel and Roberta locked hands.

They locked eyes.

They locked wills.

Their hands remained in the starting position, their arms shaking with the effort, as they battled furiously with each other.

Then, as I expected, Gretel began to force Roberta's hand down towards the ground.

But only for a moment.

Incredibly, against all odds and all known laws of probability, physics and nature, Roberta not only halted the descent, but began to push Gretel's hand back up to where they'd started, and kept on pushing until she pushed Gretel's hand over and held it down hard against the ground.

Gretel shook her head. "I can't believe it!" she said, sitting up and rubbing her wrist, as if it were sore. "Nobody but my dad has ever beaten me at arm-wrestling. Nobody! How did you do that?"

"I guess I'm stronger than you," said Roberta matter-of-factly as she stood up.

"I can't believe it," said Gretel, over and over. "I just can't believe it."

Jenny knelt and helped Gretel to her feet. "Come on," she said, "let's get you to Mrs Plaster."

Chapter 25

Ten pieces of evidence that prove beyond a doubt that Roberta is a robot

1. She has a photographic memory.
2. She has a name that sounds like "robot".
3. She knows the Dewey decimal classification system by heart.
4. She is super-serious (has no sense of humour).
5. She has no imagination.
6. She does not feel fear.
7. She has super-human intelligence.
8. She has super-human story-writing ability.
9. She has super-human drawing ability.
10. She has super-human strength.

Chapter 26

Jenny Friendly

So now Jack agreed with me and so did Gretel, but – despite the mounting evidence (*see previous chapter*) – I was still having trouble convincing Jenny. If anything, she seemed to be getting friendlier with Roberta.

The next morning, the two of them arrived at school together practically skipping arm in arm.

"Hi, Henry!" said Jenny, waving.

"Hi, Henry!" said Roberta, copying Jenny's words, voice and wave almost exactly.

"Hi!" I waved back, trying not to let on how freaked out I was. "Jenny, do you mind if I speak to you alone for a minute?"

"Why?" she asked. "Is something the matter?"

"No, of course not," I said. "Nothing's the matter. Nothing's the matter at all! In fact, I can't think of a time where nothing mattered less than it does right at this moment!"

Roberta frowned, shrugged and turned to Jenny. "What is he talking about?" she asked.

"Oh, that's just Henry being Henry," Jenny told her. "You'll get used to him after a while. I'd better see what he wants. See you in class!"

"See you in class!" mimicked Roberta as she walked off towards the classroom.

"Are you sure you know what you're doing, Jenny?" I said, once Roberta was far enough away not to hear.

"She's really nice!" said Jenny. "You've got her all wrong, Henry. I don't know why you're being so mean."

"She's a robot, that's why!"

"No, she's not!"

"Are you calling me a liar?"

"No, but you know as well as I do that you have a wild imagination."

"True enough," I said, "but I didn't imagine that mission report in her diary!"

"I'm sure there's a reasonable explanation for what you saw," said Jenny. "Maybe you misread it."

"What part of *I am a super-advanced, super-intelligent robot from the future come to cleanse*

*the world of inefficient human beings so that
we can take over the Earth* could I have misread
exactly?"

"There's no need to be sarcastic," said Jenny.
"I just find it a little bit hard to believe, that's
all. Think about it. Even if what you were
saying could be shown to be true beyond
doubt – that Roberta really *is* a super-
advanced, super-intelligent robot determined
to take over the world – why on earth would
she write it all down in her diary and leave it
where anybody could find it? That doesn't
seem to be a very super-intelligent thing to
do!"

"How would I know why she does what she
does?" I said. "I'm not a super-advanced, super-
intelligent robot. She probably doesn't even
know herself; she's most likely just following
orders. All I know is what I saw."

"Well, as far as I can see she hasn't actually
done anything evil," said Jenny. "If anything,
she's been really helpful."

"Listen to me, Jenny," I said. "She's not
helpful *or* nice . . . she's trying to lull us into a
false sense of security before she strikes!"

The first bell rang.

"I'm sorry, Henry, but you'll have to excuse

me," said Jenny, walking off. "I have to go and put a banana on Mr Brainfright's desk."

That was Jenny Friendly for you.

She was so nice and friendly that she just couldn't imagine anybody *not* being as nice and as friendly as she was.

But that was about to change.

I heard the scream from the playground.

Chapter 27

Jenny Not-So-Friendly

I ran as fast as I could to the classroom.

I bounded up the steps in one mighty leap, skidded my way down the corridor, caught hold of the door frame and looked into the room.

Jenny and Roberta were alone in there – standing on either side of Mr Brainfright's desk, facing each other.

But Jenny no longer looked like the Jenny I knew.

Her face was red. She was shaking. "I can't believe it! I just can't believe it!" she was saying over and over.

"I'm only giving Mr Brainfright some bananas," said Roberta. "I thought it was supposed to be a nice thing to do!"

On Mr Brainfright's desk there was a whole *bunch* of bananas.

"One banana is *nice*," said Jenny. "A whole bunch is just showing off! Besides, giving Mr Brainfright a banana a day is *my* idea! I thought of it first!"

Roberta stared at Jenny blankly. "I'll take them away then," she said.

"No, let me save you the trouble." And saying that, Jenny snatched the bananas off the desk and threw them out of the window.

For a moment we just stood there.

Nobody knew quite what to say.

I'd never seen Jenny Friendly do anything so *unfriendly* in her life.

Roberta looked stunned – completely baffled – by Jenny's behaviour.

"Maybe Henry's right about you!" hissed Jenny. "Maybe you're not just different. Maybe you really are a—"

I ran to her and put my hand over her mouth. "That's enough, Jenny," I said.

"No, it's not," said Roberta, her eyes steely grey. "Let her finish, Henry!"

Jenny tried her best to finish, but I managed to muffle the word I knew she was dying to throw at Roberta.

I began dragging Jenny out of the classroom as quickly as I could. "She's upset," I said to

Roberta. "She doesn't know what she's saying!"

"I think she would if you'd take your hand off her mouth," she replied.

"Are you all right, Jenny?" I said when I'd finally managed to drag her out of the room and down to the bottom of the steps.

"No!" she said, gasping for breath. "I'm *not* all right. And neither is Roberta. Not only is she super-strong, super-intelligent, and all those things you said, she's *super-nice*, too. But nobody's nicer than me, Henry. Nobody *human*, that is."

"So you agree?" I said. "You really think she's a robot?"

Jenny nodded. "Exterminating us all is one thing, but if Roberta thinks that she can be *nicer* than me, she's got another thing coming."

"Jenny," I said, "at the moment Roberta *is* nicer than you. You threw her bananas out of the window, which wasn't very nice."

Jenny put her hand to her mouth in horror as she suddenly realized what she had done. "Oh, no!" she said. "I did?"

"I'm afraid so. I think you should go and get

them for her and say sorry. We can't let her know that we're on to her. We need to act like nothing is wrong."

"Of course!" said Jenny. "I feel so awful . . . I think I owe you an apology, too."

"No, you don't," I said. "You always give people the benefit of the doubt. It's one of the many nice things about you. But at the moment it's Roberta you need to apologize to. Think you can manage it?"

Jenny gulped, closed her eyes, and softened her face into a beautiful smile. "Of course," she said. "I'm *Jenny Friendly*! If I can't do it, then *nobody* can!"

As Jenny and I returned to the classroom with the bananas, Mr Brainfright came in and sat at his desk.

"Well, I never!" he said, looking up at Jenny. "Are they for me?"

"Yes," she said. "But they're not *from* me."

Mr Brainfright frowned. "They're not?" he said. "Then who are they from?"

"Roberta," said Jenny, placing the bananas on Roberta's desk. "I'm afraid we had a bit of an accident and, well, anyway . . . here they are. Sorry, Roberta."

"That's quite OK, Jenny," she said sweetly. "Accidents happen."

"Very true words indeed," said Mr Brainfright. "Why, only this morning I accidentally mistook my jacket for my trousers, which is why I'm a little late. I put my legs into the sleeves and then couldn't walk or even get them out again. It took me quite a while to sort myself out. Don't you hate it when that happens?"

Some of us laughed, others just looked at him blankly. He was probably joking, but you couldn't always be sure with Mr Brainfright.

Roberta got up and put the bananas on Mr Brainfright's desk.

"Well, thank *you*, Roberta!" said Mr Brainfright, taking them from her. "That's *very* thoughtful! I think that's the *nicest* thing that anybody has ever done for me!"

Poor Jenny.

She was gripping the edges of her desk so hard that her knuckles were white. I was worried that she was going to launch herself across the classroom and tear Roberta's metallic body to shreds.

"Cool it, Jenny," I whispered. "Don't do anything stupid. We'll deal with it, but not right now, OK? For the moment I need you to stay *nice*."

Jenny looked at me and nodded, smiling stiffly. "I'm nice," she said through gritted teeth. "I'm *really, really, really nice*."

Chapter 28

Robot sandwiches

We kept a close watch on Roberta for the rest of the morning, but she didn't do anything suspicious. She just worked quietly and methodically. As quietly and methodically as a . . . well, you know what. Even Jenny Friendly knew by now, although I think she was still having trouble believing it.

At lunch we were sitting in our usual spot in the playground. We watched Roberta walk out into the playground and sit down on a seat by herself to eat her lunch.

"She's all alone," said Jenny. "Should I go and invite her to have lunch with us?"

"Are you kidding?" I said. "After the way she out-niced you this morning?"

"No, I suppose not," said Jenny. "I just hate seeing anybody all on their own."

"She won't be lonely for long if she gets her way," said Gretel. "She and her robot pals will soon be running this place!"

"Yikes!" said Newton.

"I said, *'if she gets her way'*, Newton. *If!*"

"She doesn't *seem* like a robot, though," said Jenny.

"Don't be fooled," I said. "That's exactly what she wants you to think."

"But she's eating a sandwich," said Jenny. "That doesn't seem like something a robot would do."

"It's not a *real* sandwich," I said. "Roberta is a super-advanced, super-intelligent robot intent on concealing her true identity. She's not going to sit there eating nuts and bolts and drinking oil like an ordinary robot. She's disguised her robot fuel to look like a regular sandwich, but it's really a *robot* sandwich. She's smart . . . really smart."

Everybody nodded. Well, everybody but Newton. "I'm frightened," he said. "I want to go home."

"But you can't," said Gretel. "It's only lunch time."

"I still want to go home," said Newton. "It will be safer there."

105

"Only for a while," I pointed out.

"What do you mean?" said Newton.

"Exterminating everyone at Northwest Southeast Central School is only the beginning. Once Roberta and her robot army are finished with us, they'll start on the whole world! You can run, but you can't hide, Newton. Better that we make a stand now rather than wait until it's too late."

Newton gulped so loudly it sounded like he was trying to swallow a baseball.

"Henry's right," said Gretel. "We need to act now. The question is, how exactly do we act? What can we do to stop her?"

"Before we can answer that question," I said, "we need to know exactly what Roberta is planning to do and when she's planning to do it."

"Yeah, but how do we find that out?" asked Jenny. "It's not like we can just go and ask her."

"Have you checked her diary lately?" said Jack. "She could have written another report. It may give us a clue."

"Of course!" I said, slamming my fist into my hand. "Why didn't I think of that?"

Jack smiled and shrugged. "I guess you're not as smart as I am."

"Or as disrespectful of somebody else's privacy," said Jenny. "You can't just go around reading other people's diaries whenever you feel like it."

"But she's a robot!" said Jack.

"Even robots are entitled to privacy," said Jenny.

"Not when they're planning to take over the world, they're not," I said.

"My mother says two wrongs don't make a right," said Jenny.

"Really?" I said. "What does your mother say about robots invading the world and exterminating all the humans . . . or, for that matter, about putting whole bunches of bananas on to a teacher's desk?"

Jenny thought for a moment and then shrugged. "I don't know. She's never really said anything about those things . . . I'll ask her tonight."

"We don't have that much time!" I said. "I say we stay behind after school and check her diary. All in favour, raise your hands."

One by one, each of us raised a hand.

Even Newton.

And, finally, Jenny.

Meanwhile, Roberta continued to eat her robot sandwich, completely oblivious to the fact that her evil plans were about to be completely undone.

Chapter 29

Reading Roberta's diary

That afternoon we waited until everyone had left the classroom, and then one by one we each snuck back in.

It was easier than I'd thought it was going to be.

Roberta had left her diary right on top of her desk.

We put Newton at the door as lookout. The rest of the gang crowded around me as I picked Roberta's diary up and opened it to Monday's entry, where she'd written her report.

I tapped the page with my finger. "Look at this!" I said.

"No," said Jenny, turning her head away. "I can't! I simply *can't* look at somebody else's diary!"

"All right, then," I said, "I'll read it to you. *My name is Robota Flywheel. I am a super-*

advanced, super-intelligent robot from the future. . ."

Jenny put her fingers in her ears – but she couldn't block the sound of my voice completely. I could tell, because as I read her eyes widened and she slowly took her fingers away from her ears. She moved over to the desk to look at what I was reading.

"Henry. . ." she gasped, ". . . this is awful. But she *does* have lovely neat handwriting. . ."

"JENNY!" I said. "Get a grip! We're not here to admire her handwriting – we're here to find out when and how she's planning to do away with us all!"

"Sorry, Henry. . ." said Jenny, who seemed to have forgotten her mother's prohibition about diary reading. "What do you think this means?"

"What?" I said.

"Here," said Jenny, pointing. "She's circled tomorrow's date and written ASSEMBLY with three exclamation marks."

"Uh-oh," I said. "I'll tell you what it means. It means that we're in *big* trouble. She's planning her robot attack for tomorrow's assembly."

"I knew it!" said Jack, slamming his fist into his hand. "I knew it all along!"

"No, you didn't," I said. "Just the other day you were ready to form the Roberta Flywheel Fan Club."

"No, I wasn't," said Jack. "I was just playing along with her so she wouldn't know that I knew what she was up to."

"I thought her stick idea was really good, though," said Newton from the doorway. "And washing the tap handles actually works! I didn't get one germ on me yesterday!"

"That's beside the point!" I said. "I don't care how innovative her ideas on playground cleaning and hand washing are: she's an evil robot who's out to destroy us all at assembly tomorrow morning! It's here in black and white!"

"Do you think she'll do it with pointy sticks?" said Newton, who had abandoned his lookout post and had joined us at the desk. "With germs on them?"

"I don't know *what* she has in mind," I said. "But I think it will be worse than germy, pointy sticks. Much worse. And what are you doing here, anyway? You're supposed to be our lookout. SO LOOK OUT!"

"Sorry, Henry," said Newton. "But I got scared over there all by myself."

"You shouldn't yell at him like that, Henry," said Jenny. "He's *scared*!"

"Well, so am I!" I said.

And a few seconds later I was terrified.

Because we heard a noise at the classroom door.

We looked up guiltily.

It was Roberta.

Chapter 30

Sprung!

"What are you doing?" said Roberta. "Why are you all around my desk? Are you reading my diary?"

"NO!" I said, slamming it shut. "I just found it on the floor and I opened it to see who it belonged to. I was just putting it back."

"Yes, that's right," said Jenny, her face going bright red. "Henry was just putting it back." She wasn't very good at lying. In fact, this was probably her first ever attempt.

"Yep, that's what happened, all right," said Jack. "Exactly what they said."

Gretel murmured her agreement.

Newton just nodded in terror.

Roberta looked at us in a way that suggested she didn't believe a word we were saying.

She started walking towards us.

We all backed slowly away.

"You're saying one thing to me," said Roberta, "but your body language is suggesting something else completely. I think you read it. You *know*, don't you?"

"Um," I said, "no . . . I don't know anything about it . . . I mean, if there was anything to know . . . which there isn't, not that I would know whether there is or there isn't anything to know . . . or not know . . . anything about!"

"I think you *do* know," said Roberta quietly. "And I'd prefer it if you didn't tell anyone. It's going to be hard enough as it is, but if everyone knows beforehand, that will make it even harder for me."

We all looked at one another in horror.

"I'm doing my best to fit in," said Roberta.

"How will doing what you're planning to do help you to fit in?" asked Jenny.

"It wasn't my idea," said Roberta. "I'm just going along with it."

"Well . . . if that's how you feel, then maybe you shouldn't do it," stammered Jenny.

"I've thought about that, believe me," said Roberta. "But I said I would and I will. There's no turning back. All I'm asking is, please don't tell anyone else."

She stepped towards us.

We stepped back.

"Please!" said Roberta. "Promise?"

"Sure!" I said. "We won't tell anyone, will we, guys?"

"NO," said Jenny, a little too loudly and blushing even brighter red than before.

"Absolutely," said Gretel. "You can count on us."

"Our lips are sealed," said Jack.

"Do you promise?" said Roberta, coming even closer. "Really?"

We were backing away fast now, nodding emphatically.

I felt the back of my knees touch the window sill. "Jump!" I said.

We all turned and jumped.

Straight out of the window!

Then we sprang up and ran.

For our lives.

Chapter 31

Grant Gadget to the rescue

We ran to the school gate and stopped there to catch our breath.

"Great," said Gretel. "So now she knows we know. We're going to have to act fast. We need a plan. Any ideas?"

Nobody said anything.

"There's nothing we can do," said Newton. "She's more advanced than us. She's more intelligent than us. She's stronger than us. There's no way we can fight a super-advanced, super-intelligent robot from the future!"

"Perhaps there is," said Jenny, narrowing her eyes. "My mother says that sometimes you need to fight fire with fire."

"I'm scared of fire," muttered Newton.

"No, it means fight *like* with *like*," Jenny explained. "We're fighting a robot so we *need* a robot to help us."

"Great idea, Jenny," said Gretel. "But where are we going to get a robot from?"

"Grant Gadget, of course!" I said.

"No," groaned Jack. "Not Grant. We need a robot that actually works."

"Don't be mean, Jack," said Jenny. "I think Grant is really clever."

"Yeah," I said. "Plus he's the only person I can think of who might be able to help us. Does anybody have a better idea?"

"No, but Grant's inventions never work," said Jack.

"That's not true," said Jenny. "They work *sometimes*."

"Yeah," said Jack. "And then they blow up!"

"They don't *always* blow up," said Jenny.

"You're right," said Jack. "Sometimes smoke comes out of them and they emit a high-pitched noise . . . and *then* they blow up."

"Fair point," I said. "But the question is: do you have a better idea?"

Jack thought for a minute. Then shrugged. "No."

We ran to Grant's house as fast as we could.

When we got there, his mother sent us out the back to his father's workshop.

He was pretty surprised to see us, but nowhere near as surprised as he was once we'd told him all about what we'd discovered.

"So," I said once we'd finished filling him in, "can you build a robot capable of stopping Roberta?"

"I'm pretty sure I could," said Grant. "As a matter of fact, my dad has been doing some very interesting work on AI lately. And I've been helping him with it."

"What does AI mean?" asked Newton. "It sounds scary."

"It means Artificial Intelligence," Grant explained. "As in robots. Dad's away at an AI conference at the moment, which is lucky because it means I can use his workshop to build whatever I want."

"So you really could build a robot?" said Jenny. "That would be great."

"Yeah, fantastic," said Gretel.

"Way to go, Grant," I said, clapping him on the back.

"Yay! Great!" said Jack. But he was being sarcastic.

"What sort of features would you like it to have?" Grant said, ignoring Jack.

"We can choose?" asked Jenny, excitedly.

"Eye colour? Hair colour? That sort of thing?"

"No," said Grant, rolling his eyes. "I meant what sort of robot do you want? There are lots of different types, you know. Household robots, nano-bots, marine-bots, fighting robots—"

"A *fighting* robot!" said Gretel.

"Yeah. We definitely need a fighting robot!" I said. "A *robot*-fighting robot."

Grant stroked his chin. "Let me get some details." He took a small pen and notepad out of his shirt pocket. "Now, let's see . . . do you want it to have laser beam eyes?"

"What colour are they?" asked Jenny.

"Red when activated," said Grant. "The laser beams incinerate everything the robot looks at."

"Wow!" said Jack. "They sound pretty cool!" This time he wasn't being sarcastic.

"No!" said Newton. "I'm scared of laser beam eyes."

"They do sound a bit dangerous," I said. "We don't want anyone getting hurt. We just want to stop Roberta."

"I guess you're right," said Grant. "I suppose that rules out flame-thrower hands as well?"

"Yes," I said.

"I'll give it an ultra-high-frequency enemy-robot jammer," said Grant. "That's what my dad's been working on. It's very effective."

"What does it do?" I asked.

"It emits an extremely high-frequency pulse that scrambles the enemy robot's circuits," said Grant. "It can also shatter glass, but that's less useful."

"An extremely high-frequency pulse," said Jack. "I'd like to hear that."

"You can't," said Grant. "It's too high for the human ear to hear. Only robots – and dogs – can hear it."

"I kinda figured that," said Jack. "I was joking."

"Oh," said Grant. "Well, very funny. But getting back to the situation at hand. Do you want the robot to be able to turn into a submarine?"

"Can you do that?" said Gretel.

"I think so," said Grant. "And does it need to be able to travel into space?"

"It could be really handy if a chase situation develops," I said. "We don't know what Roberta is capable of."

"Done," said Grant. "Anything else?"

"I don't know," I said. "Just give it anything else you think it would need to be able to protect the Earth against a robot uprising."

Grant nodded. "In that case, I'd really recommend the flame-thrower hands."

"OK," I said. "As long as they don't burn everybody."

"No, I promise," said Grant. "I'll get straight on it!"

"Great!" I said. "How soon can you have it ready?"

"Shouldn't take me too long at all," said Grant. "I reckon if all the materials I need are available and everything goes according to plan, I should have it ready, hmmm, let me see . . . by the end of the year."

"WHAT!?" we all cried.

"Is there a problem?" said Grant.

"Yes," I said. "We can't wait that long!"

"Why, when do you need it by?"

"TOMORROW MORNING!" I said. "At the very latest! We're pretty sure she's planning something for the school assembly."

Grant nodded. "I see," he said, taking this new information in. "That doesn't give me much time."

"Can you do it?" I said.

"I guess it's *possible*," said Grant, "but I may not be able to include all the features you wanted. Like submarine capabilities, for instance. That's pretty complicated."

"Don't worry about it," I said. "The only water close to us is Northwest Lake, which is really just a big puddle. Can we still have space travel, though? Interplanetary robot-chases are quite common."

"Of course!" said Grant. "Space travel is a standard feature on all my robots."

"How many have you made?" Gretel asked.

"This will be the first," said Grant. "But if this works, I'll probably build a lot more."

"*If* it works?" said Jack. "What do you mean *if* it works?"

But Grant wasn't listening. He had his head down and was scribbling away. "I'll see you all tomorrow," he mumbled. "Let's meet at the front gate half an hour before school starts."

We all looked at one another. It was obviously time to leave.

"Do you think he can really do it?" asked Newton once we were back out on the street.

"He has to," I said. "It's the only hope we've got."

"Well, that's it then," said Jack. "We are definitely doomed."

Chapter 32

Grantbot 1000

I got to school early the next day and met up with the others at the gate.

"Where's Grant?" asked Newton, shivering as dark storm clouds massed overhead.

"I don't know," I said. "He was supposed to be here."

"Do you think everything's all right?" said Jenny.

"I hope so," I said. "It has to be. The future of humankind depends on it."

I looked up at the clouds.

There was going to be a storm. That was for sure.

"Here he is!" said Newton.

Grant was hurrying across the playground towards us.

"Well," said Jack. "Have you got it?"

"Yes," said Grant, his eyes shining with excitement.

"Where is it?" said Gretel, looking all around.

"It's down behind Mr Spade's workshop," said Grant. "I walked it to school really early so nobody would see. We've been here for a while. Come and check it out!"

Grant hurried off without waiting for us. We ran after him.

We followed him around to the back of Mr Spade's shed, where there was a large object covered in a sheet of blue plastic.

"Are you ready?" said Grant. "Prepare to lay your eyes on the eighth wonder of the world: the GRANTBOT 1000!"

With a dramatic flourish, Grant swept the sheet of plastic away, revealing a large home-made but terrifying-looking robot.

It towered over us. It was made up of different sorts of metal all riveted and welded together. It had a big bucket-shaped metal head with a rectangular slot for eyes and a single antenna sticking out the top. Its arms were long metal tubes with big shiny steel claws bolted on to the end. Its legs were made of the same metal tubing as the arms – only thicker – and it was wearing a pair of knee-high black wellies.

"Wow!" said Jenny. "That is *really* something, Grant! You've done a great job."

"Yeah," said Gretel. "It looks extremely powerful."

"I'm scared!" said Newton.

"That's the idea," said Grant.

"Why is it wearing wellies?" Jack asked.

"I was going to build a pair of jet boots for space travel," said Grant, "but I ran out of time."

"Well, it *is* going to rain today," said Jenny, "so it's a good thing he has them – they will keep his feet dry."

"Great!" said Jack. "So it can't go underwater or fly into space, but it *can* step into puddles. Does it at least have flame-thrower hands?"

"Unfortunately not," said Grant. "I had an accident while I was trying to install them and almost burned down my dad's workshop."

"We should have known," said Jack, rolling his eyes and shaking his head. "This robot doesn't actually work, does it? It's just a big toy."

"I'll let you be the judge of that," said Grant. He turned to the Grantbot and said, "Grantbot, pick up the small human immediately to your right!"

And then an amazing thing happened.

Grant's giant robot came to life.

There was a loud whirring sound, followed by three sharp beeps. A blazing beam of light shot out of the opening in the front of its head. The robot turned towards Jack, who stood there blinking, and scooped him up in its powerful arms.

We all gasped.

Newton hid behind Jenny.

"Let me go!" yelled Jack.

"Just a big toy, eh?" said Grant.

"I take it back! It's the best robot ever! You're a genius, Grant! Now make it let me go!"

"Grantbot!" commanded Grant. "Let him go!"

The Grantbot obeyed Grant's order instantly. It opened its arms and Jack fell to the ground with a thud.

"Hmmm," said Grant. "I think I probably should have said 'Put him down gently'."

Jack got up, rubbing his back. I was expecting him to be mad, but he wasn't. "I've underestimated you, Grant," he said. "That is SO cool! Could you make me one?"

"How about we just get on with saving the world for the moment?" I said.

"Yeah," said Grant. "I'd prefer not to take any orders until we get that sorted out. How long before the assembly?"

"About fifteen minutes . . . and counting," I said.

"I'll just do some systems checks and then we'll be ready to go!" Grant opened a hatch on the front of the Grantbot's chest to reveal a control panel and began tinkering.

Chapter 33

A little problem

I was getting restless. We could see students and teachers heading towards the assembly hall.

Grant had been fiddling with the Grantbot's control panel for what felt like hours.

"Are you ready yet?" I said. "The assembly starts soon."

Grant didn't answer me. He was deep in concentration.

"That's strange," he mumbled.

"What?" I said. "What's strange?"

"One of the central command modules is failing to respond."

"Well, make it respond," I said. "We really have to get going now."

Grant looked up from the control panel and stared at me. "Henry," he said, "there's a little problem."

"What?"

"It's not working."

"I wouldn't call that a *little* problem, Grant," said Jack. "I'd say that's more of a BIG problem. A REALLY BIG problem."

"I know, I know," said Grant, turning back to the Grantbot's control panel. "But I just don't know what's wrong. I can't fix it. I was running a test on the high-frequency enemy-robot signal jammer and for some reason it's short-circuited the whole system."

"I knew it was too good to be true," said Jack. "As if this was actually going to work!"

"Being negative is not going to help," said Jenny. "Is there anything we can do, Grant?"

"Do you want me to give it a thump?" Gretel offered. "That always works on our TV."

Grant shook his head and fiddled some more with the Grantbot's control panel. "I don't understand it. . ." he mumbled.

I didn't understand either, but then I never understood much of Grant's technobabble. "What are we going to do?" I said, pulling at my hair and pacing around. I was starting to panic. The Grantbot was all we had, and if that wasn't working, we had . . . well . . . nothing. We were doomed.

Roberta and her robot buddies would take over the world.

And what would become of us?

What did Roberta mean by "exterminate", exactly?

Did she mean exterminate us for ever, or did she mean exterminate our human identities and turn us into robot slaves? Would there be a *Henrybot* who looked like me, talked like me, told stories like me . . . only better?

I didn't want the world to be taken over by robots. The funny thing was that when I was younger I used to really *like* robots. In fact, I used to make myself robot costumes all the time. I would spend whole days dressed as a robot, acting like a robot, talking like a robot. I'd even try to sleep standing up because I figured that's how robots would sleep. I'd always wake up once I hit the floor, of course, but that's how much I loved playing robots. And I did have a box on my head to soften the blow.

Then I had an idea.

A crazy one, sure, but at least it was an idea.

I turned back to look at Grant.

"Any luck?" I said, though I already knew the answer.

"No, I'm sorry, Henry," said Grant. "I'm really sorry. I just can't figure out what's wrong. I'll keep working on it though."

I patted Grant on the shoulder. "I'm sorry, too," I said, "but thanks for trying . . . it almost worked."

"Well, I guess that's it," said Jack, shrugging gloomily. "It's all over. Roberta has won. So long, everyone . . . it's been nice knowing you."

"Maybe not," I said.

"What?!" said Jack. "Are you saying it hasn't been nice knowing me?"

"No – I mean maybe it's not all over. Not yet."

"What are you talking about, Henry?" said Jenny.

"We've got to get to the art room . . . fast!"

"The art room?" said Jack. "At a time like this? The school is about to be attacked by a super-advanced, super-intelligent robot, and all you can think about is finger painting?"

"I didn't say anything about finger painting," I said. "I was thinking more along the lines of a making a robot-fighting robot . . . only this time not an *actual* one, a replica! Of course, we won't be able to fight Roberta, but if we make it convincing enough, hopefully she won't be able to tell the difference and we can bluff her into calling off her attack."

"Are you out of your mind?" said Jack. "The assembly starts in five minutes! How can we possibly build a robot-fighting robot replica in that short a time?"

"Because we have to," I said. "We just have to."

Chapter 34

How to transform yourself into a convincing robot-fighting robot replica in five minutes or less

THINGS YOU WILL NEED
- *Yourself*
- *Your friends*
- *1 large roll of silver duct tape*
- *1 large cardboard box*
- *1 small cardboard box*
- *1 roll of aluminium foil*
- *1 white plastic tray*
- *3 bottle tops*
- *1 sponge and a bowl of soapy water*
- *2 hairspray cans*
- *2 pipe cleaners*
- *1 pair of scissors*
- *2 barbecue tongs*

PROCEDURE

1. *Go to Mrs Rainbow's art room. If you haven't been able to find any of the things on the list, you'll definitely find them here. (Mrs Rainbow's art room has everything!)*

2. *Cut a hole (big enough to put your head through) in the top of the large box.*

3. *Cut an arm hole on each side.*

4. *Put your head through the head hole and your arms through the arm holes.*

5. *Put the small box on your head.*

6. *Grab a pair of scissors and make eye holes so that you can see out.*

7. *Make eye holes carefully!!! If you feel sharp, stabbing pains in your eyes, you're probably not being quite careful enough.*

8. *With the box on your head, draw a scary robot face on to the front. Get Jack to do this. Not only is he the best drawer – well, apart from Roberta, of course – but you've got a box on your head.*

9. *At this point you will need to calm Newton down because he will be a bit freaked out by the scary robot face that Jack just drew. Get Jenny to do this because she's really good at calming Newton down.*

10. *Wrap silver duct tape around the gaps*

between the head and arm holes and your body so it looks like your entire body is made of metal. I would suggest that you get Gretel to do this rather than Jack because he tends to get a little carried away with duct tape and, later, when you really need to get your robot-fighting robot-replica suit off, *you won't be able to*.

11. *Wrap aluminium foil around all parts of your body that don't have duct tape wrapped around them.*

12. *Make an authentic-looking control panel by glueing three bottle tops on to a white plastic tray and sticking it on the front of your body.*

13. *Make an authentic-looking jet-pack by attaching two upside-down hairspray cans (without their lids) to the back of your body.*

14. *Make an authentic-looking set of robot antennae by taping a pipe cleaner on each side of your head. (Don't let Newton do the taping. He's not only hopeless with tape but he's scared of pipe cleaners.)*

15. *Put a pair of barbecue tongs in your left hand and secure them with lots and lots of silver duct tape. This will be your left robot claw.*

16. *Get Jenny to do the same thing with another set of barbecue tongs to your right hand. (You need help with this because these robot claws look great but it's impossible to do anything with your hands – except clack the tongs menacingly – once they are on.)*

17. *Use whatever silver duct tape you have left over to fortify your body, head, arms, legs, feet and robot claws.*

18. *Get Jenny to reassure Newton that you're not really a robot-fighting robot, you're just a fully functioning, completely convincing robot-fighting robot replica.*

19. *Congratulations! You are now a fully functioning, completely convincing robot-fighting robot replica.*

20. *Good luck!*

Chapter 35

Henrybot to the rescue!

I looked at myself in one of the many mosaic mirrors hanging around the room.

But I wasn't me any more.

I was a robot.

Sure, I didn't look as scary as the Grantbot 1000, but I did look good.

Good enough to call Roberta's bluff . . . or so I hoped.

"Not bad," said Jack admiringly. "Not bad at all. If I didn't know that you were Henry McThrottle dressed up as a robot-fighting robot, I'd definitely think that you were a robot-fighting robot!"

"Let's hope Roberta feels the same way," said Gretel.

"What-are-you-talk-ing-a-bout?" I said in my best robo-speak. "I-AM-a-ro-bot-fight-ing-ro-bot!"

"Yikes!" said Newton. "I'm scared of robots!"

"It's OK, Newton," said Jenny, patiently. "It's not really a robot, remember? It's just Henry dressed up in a robot costume."

Newton nodded uncertainly. "I know," he said, "but I'm scared of robots AND of people dressed up in robot costumes!"

"I-am-not-a-per-son-dressed-up-in-a-ro-bot-COST-UME," I said. "I-am-a-Hen-ry-bot-1000."

"Yikes!" said Newton, sprinting for the door. "Run!"

"Henry!" said Jenny, shaking her head. "Stop speaking like that! You're scaring Newton!"

"Speak-ing-like-what?" I said.

"Like a robot," said Jenny.

"But-I-am-a-ro. . ."

"Henry!" said Jenny.

"OK, OK," I said. "Just practising my voice – I don't have much time, you know!"

The bell rang.

"No time at all, actually," said Jack. "We'd better get you to the assembly. Hurry!"

"Af-fir-ma-tive," I said, turning myself – with difficulty – towards the door.

It wasn't easy to turn in my new robot costume.

And it was even harder to walk with all the foil and duct tape wrapped around my legs. I found this out the hard way. I took a step forward . . . and fell flat on my face.

"Uh-oh," said Gretel. "Our robot has fallen over!"

"Not a promising start," said Jack.

"I-am-do-ing-my-best," I said. "Can-you-help-me-up?"

"Affirmative," said Jack, lifting me up and putting my arm across his shoulder.

I hobbled across the playground as fast as I could.

But it wasn't fast enough.

As we got close to the building a round of applause was just dying down . . . and then I heard Roberta's voice booming from the hall.

"I am a super-advanced, super-intelligent robot from the future. I have been sent here by my masters to cleanse the world of inefficient human beings so that we can take over the Earth."

I didn't need to hear any more.

I already knew the rest.

They were the same words she had written in her diary.

There was no time to waste.

Chapter 36

Henrybot versus Robota

I burst into the assembly hall.

Roberta was standing on the stage, reading aloud about her plans for world domination.

How she planned to do this I wasn't exactly sure, but I did know one thing: she wasn't going to get away with it.

"STOP-RIGHT-THERE!" I commanded in the most threatening robot voice I could possibly muster.

Roberta did stop right there. She stared at me in open-mouthed astonishment, as did Mr Greenbeard, who was sitting on the stage to her right.

The whole school now turned to watch me as I moved stiffly up the centre aisle and climbed the five steps to the stage with great difficulty.

"You're not going to get away with this as easily as you think," I said. "You're not the only

142

robot in this town, you know. Unless you come quietly, I will be forced to unleash my terrifying robot power on you. I will show no mercy!"

Roberta, Mr Greenbeard and the rest of the school continued to stare at me. It was clear they'd never seen a robot quite as impressive as me before.

"Who are you?" said Mr Greenbeard, rising to his feet. "Identify yourself, sailor!"

"I am no sailor," I assured Mr Greenbeard. "I am one of an army of ten thousand robot-fighting robots stationed outside this assembly hall ready to attack at my command unless Robota surrenders right now and gives up her evil plans of robot domination for ever!"

Roberta still looked stunned. She clearly hadn't been expecting any resistance. This had really thrown a wrench in her works. Our plan was working perfectly.

Then she said something that I was definitely not expecting.

"Henry?"

She peered in at me through my eye holes.

"Is that you in there?"

I couldn't believe it.

She'd seen through my disguise!

But then, I supposed, I shouldn't have been

so surprised. After all she *was* a super-intelligent robot with super-human powers of observation. But I still had a few tricks of my own.

I clacked my barbecue tongs at her. "I AM NOT HENRY. I AM A ROBOT-FIGHTING ROBOT!"

"I thought you might be a bit upset. . ." said Roberta.

"A little bit upset?" I said. "I'm more than a little bit upset!"

"I can see that," said Roberta, "but I didn't think you'd go this far."

"Oh, you've underestimated me," I said. "I'll do whatever it takes to defend the world against your evil plans!"

"What evil plans?" said Roberta. "All I'm doing is reading my story out like Mr Brainfright asked me to. I know my story isn't as good as the ones you write, but I don't really think the world is in any danger!"

"Story?" I said. "What are you talking about?"

"My robot story," said Roberta.

"Huh?"

Roberta sighed impatiently. "My robot story," she said. "The one I wrote for my creative

144

writing piece. I caught you reading my first draft, remember?"

"I read your *diary*," I said.

"Yes, that's what I mean," said Roberta. "I wrote the first draft in my diary."

"That was a *story*?" I said.

"*Of course!*" said Roberta.

"So you're *not actually* a robot?" I said.

"No," said Roberta, starting to giggle. "I'm no more of a robot than you are . . . though that is an excellent costume!"

Roberta wasn't the only one who was giggling. I looked out into the hall. The entire school was laughing, including the teachers, and – worst of all – Jack, Jenny, Gretel and Newton.

I didn't know what to think.

Either I had just made the stupidest mistake of my life . . . or Roberta's claim that her report was a made-up story was just another one of her super-intelligent strategies to deflect attention from the truth that she really was a robot.

"I told you it was a powerful piece, Roberta," said Mr Brainfright, coming up on to the stage, his eyes wet from laughing.

That's when I had the answer to my question.

I'd just made the stupidest mistake of my life.

"Roberta wrote a monologue from the point of view of a futuristic robot invader," explained Mr Brainfright, "and it was so good I suggested that she read it out at the assembly."

So that was why she'd circled today as the big day!

"Why didn't you tell me?" I said to Roberta.

"I was feeling nervous about reading in front of the whole school. I didn't want anyone to know about it beforehand. I thought that would make it worse," she said. "But I thought you knew. I caught you reading the notes I'd made in my diary!"

"We thought it was an actual mission report written by a robot!" I said. "And that you planned to exterminate us all during the assembly."

"You thought I was making plans to take over the world?"

"Yes," I admitted, "I guess that's what I – I mean *we* – thought."

My answer triggered a fresh wave of laughter from the audience.

Roberta broke down giggling.

It was humiliating, but in a weird way, even though it was at my expense, it was good to see

Roberta actually laughing and enjoying herself like everybody else.

And, of course, it was much better than being exterminated by robots.

But above all, it was *DEFINITELY* better than what happened next.

Chapter 37

Grantbot versus Henrybot

Suddenly, there was a huge crash at the back of the hall.

I turned around as quickly as I could ... which wasn't very quick, but quick enough to see the Grantbot come crashing through the doorway, splintering the door frame and crumbling the brickwork around it.

That sure wiped the smiles off everybody's faces.

"I said *open it first* and *then go through it*!" said Grant, running behind it.

"What on earth is that?" said Roberta as the enormous Grantbot clanked and stomped its way down the middle of the hall.

"It's a Grantbot 1000!" I said.

Kids were scattering and diving for cover as it approached, its big bucket head swivelling from side to side as if scanning the room for something – robots, most likely.

"Great costume!" said Roberta. "Who's inside it?'

"Nobody . . . it's a real robot," I said. "But it broke down!"

"Well, it doesn't look like it's broken down now."

I leaned into the microphone. "Turn it off, Grant," I said. "We don't need it. Roberta's not a robot. And this is me, Henry, in this costume. Shut it off."

The Grantbot turned its big bucket head and looked directly at me. That's when I noticed its antenna had begun to pulsate red.

"Henry?" said Grant. "That's you in there?"

"Yes!" I said. "I dressed up as a robot to stand in for the Grantbot!"

"Uh-oh," said Grant. "The Grantbot thinks you're a robot!"

"Well call it off!"

"STOP, GRANTBOT!" commanded Grant. "ABORT ANTI-ROBOT MISSION. REPEAT. ABORT MISSION!"

But the Grantbot's only response was to begin walking towards the stage again.

"Grant! Shut it down!"

"I COMMAND YOU TO STOP!" said Grant,

standing in front of the Grantbot waving his arms.

But the Grantbot's only response was to pick Grant up and move him out of the way.

Students and teachers were now rushing to the doors in a blind panic as the Grantbot continued its march towards the stage, crashing through the empty chairs that the audience had deserted.

Clive Durkin wasn't fast enough. The Grantbot kicked his chair out of the way with Clive still on it. He went sprawling on to the floor.

"I'm going to tell my brother you did that!" said Clive, rolling out of the way just in time to avoid being stomped on. But the Grantbot did not appear to care about Clive, his brother, or anything else for that matter, apart from marching towards the stage.

"I can't stop it," called Grant, running after it. "It's not responding. Once it goes into robot-attack mode, it won't stop until the enemy robot is neutralized."

"But there IS no robot," I said.

"No," said Roberta. "But you're dressed like one. Obviously, it can't tell the difference."

I started clawing at my costume trying to get

it off, but it was no use. The gang had got a bit too carried away with Mrs Rainbow's silver duct tape. It was going to take hours to get this off.

"I can't get it off!" I was really panicking now. "What am I going to do?"

"Get out of here, and quick." Roberta stepped in front of me, shielding me from the Grantbot and pushing me towards the edge of the stage.

"RUN, HENRY!" she yelled.

I stumbled, fell off the stage, and crashed down on to the floor below.

I was lying there, flailing around, trying to get up, when Jenny, Jack and Gretel appeared. Roberta leaped down from the stage and all four of them helped me to my feet and began dragging me towards one of the exits.

I looked around. Everybody else, except for Mr Greenbeard, had already run from the hall.

The Grantbot thundered after us, crushing chairs under its powerful feet.

Mr Greenbeard stepped up in front of it and drew a cutlass from his side. "AVAST, YOU DOG," he shouted, "un-board this ship right now or I'll redden the decks with your black-hearted blood!"

The Grantbot, however, just knocked Mr Greenbeard aside and kept right on after me.

Mr Greenbeard looked up at the enormous back of the Grantbot as it walked away from him. "What sort of man are you?" he said, shaking his head in wonder.

"It's not a man!" I said. "It's a robot!"

"A rowboat?" said Mr Greenbeard. "Rowboats don't have legs!"

"Not a *rowboat*," I yelled, "a *robot*!" and immediately wished I hadn't because the Grantbot heard me and came crashing its way towards me.

"RUN!" Roberta cried.

I didn't need to be told again.

I ran as quickly as my duct-taped legs would allow me, which wasn't much more than a fast hobble.

Chapter 38

The most important lesson I have ever learned in my whole life

If you're going to dress up as a robot, don't use too much silver duct tape in case a robot-fighting robot sees you and you need to get out of your robot costume in a hurry.

Chapter 39

Spade attack

Roberta and I, followed closely by Mr Greenbeard, were the last ones out of the hall.

The rest of the school was standing in a huge terrified huddle outside.

As we emerged, there was a flash of lightning followed by an enormous clap of thunder.

But it wasn't just the air around us that was trembling.

The ground itself was shaking as the Grantbot attempted to smash its way out of the hall.

That's when the windows began to shatter.

"Hey!" said Grant, with excitement. "Looks like the enemy-robot frequency jammer works after all! The super-high-pitched frequency is breaking the glass. If you were a robot, you'd really be in trouble now."

"In case you hadn't noticed," I said, "I AM

really in trouble now! I'm being chased by a robot-attacking robot!"

"Make it stop, Grant!" said Jenny.

"I can't!" he said. "It won't respond to voice commands. And I can't get close enough to operate its manual control panel."

"How long before it runs out of power?" said Roberta.

"That will never happen," said Grant. "It's solar powered. Theoretically, it can run for ever."

"For ever?" said Jenny.

"It won't stop until it neutralizes the enemy robot," said Grant.

Everyone looked at me.

"We've got to get you out of that costume, Henry," said Jenny, frantically pulling at the layers of tape plastered around my arms and legs.

"WATCH OUT!" yelled Grant.

The Grantbot came crashing through the assembly hall wall . . . by pushing the entire wall over.

The wall crumbled to the ground – and then all the other walls fell down, too, and the roof collapsed. A cloud of dust and debris engulfed us.

Mr Greenbeard shook his fist at the Grantbot. "You villain!" he cried. "Just wait until I get my hands on you!"

The Grantbot stood, scanned, locked on to me, and began walking in my direction.

Mr Greenbeard strode to meet it.

"No, you don't, Mr Greenbeard!" said Jenny, grabbing his arm. "Gretel! Help me!"

"Come on, Mr Greenbeard," said Gretel. "We have to go!"

"I'm not going anywhere!" said Mr Greenbeard. "A captain *never* abandons his ship!"

"When it's being destroyed by a robot he does!" said Gretel, scooping him up in her powerful arms and throwing him over her shoulders in a fireman's lift. She hurried off with him, deposited him with the crowd of students and teachers huddled outside the school gate, and then came running back.

Mr Brainfright, meanwhile, was attempting to calm everybody down. "Relax!" he said, bravely holding his ground as the Grantbot advanced towards him. "There's no need to panic! Robots are our friends!" Then he turned to the robot. "I come in peace, my robot brother!"

As he said this, the Grantbot stopped in front of Mr Brainfright and extended its arm.

"See?" said Mr Brainfright. "He doesn't want to hurt us."

Mr Brainfright extended his right hand forward in a spirit of friendship.

The Grantbot, however, had other plans. It took Mr Brainfright's hand, picked him up, and flipped him through the air until he landed head first in a flower bed.

"What do you think you're doing, Brainfright?" said an enraged Mr Spade, appearing out of nowhere.

"This wasn't *my* idea," said Mr Brainfright, brushing dirt off his head. "In case you hadn't noticed, we're under robot attack here!"

"Robot attack?" said Mr Spade, turning around to face the Grantbot. "That heap of nuts and bolts. Nothing my spade can't fix!"

"I wouldn't do that if I were you," said Mr Brainfright.

But it was too late.

Mr Spade ran at the Grantbot, his spade raised high in the air, and then he brought it down hard across the Grantbot's shoulder.

A shower of sparks flew from the Grantbot's metal shell.

"Gotcha!" cried Mr Spade in triumph. But his victory was short-lived.

The Grantbot snatched the spade from his hands and snapped it in half like a toothpick, throwing both pieces to the ground.

Mr Spade just stood and stared.

Then he ran.

Jenny helped Mr Brainfright to his feet. "I thought you said robots were our friends!"

"They are!" said Mr Brainfright. "Except for the unfriendly ones!"

Chapter 40

Mr Brainfright's important non-joke-based lesson no. 2

Robots are our friends ... except for the unfriendly ones.

Chapter 41

Search and destroy

"Come on, Henry," said Roberta. "Run!" She grabbed my hand and dragged me along. I couldn't see a lot because of my robot mask, but I could see we were going in the direction of the art room. Jack, Jenny, Grant, Gretel and Newton were all doing their best to help me along, although Newton's assistance was mainly confined to screaming, "It's following us!" and "Help! We're all going to die!"

"Newton," said Jack, "you're not exactly helping!"

"Don't be mean, Jack!" said Jenny. "He's doing the best he can!"

"How on earth is screaming, 'Help! We're all going to die!' actually *helping* us?" said Jack.

"It makes us run faster," said Gretel.

"All very well for you to say," I said.

It was a relief to finally reach the art room.

It was even more of a relief to see Mrs Rainbow's friendly smiling face waiting to greet us at the door.

"Ah, there you are, children!" she beamed. "What a wonderful robot costume you've made! So nice to see you taking the initiative to be creative all by yourselves!"

"We're not being creative!" yelled Newton. "We're all going to die!"

Mrs Rainbow smiled. "Oh, Newton," she said, affectionately patting his head, "you do have a vivid imagination!"

"It's not my imagination, Mrs Rainbow!" he shrieked, pointing back towards the Grantbot.

Mrs Rainbow gasped. "You're wrong, Newton! It takes a lot of imagination to make a costume like that!"

"It's not a costume!" said Grant, looking a little miffed. "It's an actual working robot-fighting robot! I designed and built it myself!"

"I wouldn't actually be boasting about that, Grant," said Jack, "given that it's in the process of destroying the entire school."

"You are SO jealous!" said Grant. "Just because I can make robot-fighting robots and you can't!"

"We are all talented and creative in our

own way," said Mrs Rainbow. "There's no need to be jealous of one another. Speaking of which, why don't you ask your robot if it would like to come in and create something of its own?"

Unfortunately for Mrs Rainbow, the Grantbot was not as interested in being creative as it was in destroying me and whatever was stopping it from getting to me, which in this case was Mrs Rainbow's art room.

The Grantbot stopped, and it must have sent out a high-frequency blast because all the windows shattered, raining glass all around us. The shards arranged themselves in a surprisingly pretty pattern on the floor.

"Wonderful!" enthused Mrs Rainbow. "Simply wonderful!"

She didn't think what happened next was so wonderful, though.

The Grantbot began smashing its way into the room, knocking bricks, cracking timber and raining plaster dust down on top of us.

"Now, see here," said Mrs Rainbow, "I'm all for people expressing themselves, but not if it puts others in danger."

But the Grantbot was not interested in Mrs Rainbow's opinions on artistic expression. It picked her up and dropped her out of the window.

She got up and looked through the empty window at us. "Don't worry, children," she said. "I'll go and get help." And away she ran.

The Grantbot started towards us.

"Time to go, everyone!" said Roberta, picking me up and making a mighty leap through one of the empty window frames.

Roberta and I landed in a sprawling heap outside. The others piled out on top of us, just as the rest of the room collapsed in the same way the assembly hall had.

"Thanks, Roberta," I said. "I owe you one. But isn't exiting a building through a window against school rules?"

"Yes, and I'm not proud of it," said Roberta, climbing off the top of me and helping me up. "But I had no choice. And, besides, you know what they say – rules are made to be broken!"

The Grantbot crashed through what remained of the art room wall and came stomping after us.

"Help!" yelled Newton. "We're all going to die!"

With a combination of pushing, pulling and

carrying, the group rushed me towards the library. But before we could get inside, Mr Shush appeared.

"Not so fast," he said, standing between us and the door. "You don't just come running in here like that! This is a library, not a gymnasium! There are a few rules you need to know before you enter my library!"

"We already know them!" said Roberta, pushing her way past Mr Shush. "Besides, you know what they say!"

"No, what's that?" said Mr Shush.

"Rules are made to broken!" she said, motioning us all to follow her.

"Déjà vu!" said Jack.

"Come on!" yelled Roberta. "What are you waiting for?"

The truth was we were a little bit scared of entering the library without Mr Shush's permission, but then we were a LOT more scared of the Grantbot.

We ran inside the library.

Mr Shush didn't have time to worry about us, though ... he had to deal with the Grantbot, who was crashing up the stairs behind us.

"Not so fast," we heard him saying to the

gigantic robot. "There are a few rules you need to know before you enter my library. . ."

The Grantbot was no more interested in Mr Shush's rules than we usually were. It picked him up and deposited him head first in the book return chute.

"Number one!" came Mr Shush's muffled voice from inside the chute. "No depositing the librarian head first in the book return chute!"

The Grantbot's only response was to start smashing the library doors apart.

"Number two!" continued Mr Shush. "No smashing the library doors apart!"

I have to admit that I was pretty impressed by Mr Shush's commitment to reciting his list of rules despite the fact that he had been placed head first in the library return chute.

I was also pretty impressed by the Grantbot's commitment to destroying the enemy robot: I just wished that the "enemy robot" in this instance wasn't me.

The Grantbot demolished the library doors with one last almighty crash and blasted right on in . . . stomping all over the books as it approached.

"Oh, dear," said Jack. "I don't think Mr

Shush is going to like that. Stomping on books is *definitely* against the rules. Even I feel a little sorry for the books."

"Yikes!" said Newton.

As the library began to shake and the windows began to shatter, we ran to a window and climbed out. We made our way across the playground to the administration building and up the stairs to the school office.

We slammed the door shut and crouched down, peering out through the small window in the top half of the door.

"What do we do now?" said Jack.

"Ready ourselves for death!" yelled Newton.

"I wasn't asking you!" said Jack.

"There's nothing we can do," said Grant. "The Grantbot is programmed to search for and destroy other robots, and that's what it will do until it finds one. Unfortunately, in this case, that's Henry."

"I wasn't asking you, either!" said Jack. "It's all your fault we're in this mess!"

"You asked me to build it!"

"Well, you could have said no!"

"Jack!" said Jenny. "I know we're being chased by a terrifying robot who won't respond to Grant's commands, but that's no reason to be rude! You should apologize to both Newton *and* Grant."

Jack shrugged. "Sorry, Newton," he said. "Sorry, Grant. I'm just trying to figure out how to help Henry."

"We all are," said Jenny, "but we won't solve it by fighting amongst ourselves."

"We can't keep running," I said. "Grant's right. It's obvious that it's going to tear apart the whole school until it finds me."

"Maybe Mrs Cross will save you," said Roberta.

"What are you talking about?" I said.

"See for yourself," she said, pointing out the window – which, amazingly, hadn't been shattered.

The Grantbot had been heading towards us, but halfway across the playground, Mrs Cross had stepped in front of it.

The rest of the school, who were gathered outside the front fence, cheered.

Mrs Cross was the crossest teacher in the school. Her crossness was terrifying. If anybody could stop the Grantbot, she could.

"What do you think you're doing?" she demanded crossly. "Stop this instant!"

As she said this she stomped her foot and crossed her arms defiantly.

The Grantbot's only response was to copy her. It crossed its arms and stomped on the ground hard. So hard in fact that a huge crack opened up in the middle of the basketball court and Mrs Cross slipped and fell into it.

"Right, you've made me REALLY CROSS now," she yelled from inside the crack. "If you thought I was cross before, just wait until I get out of here!"

"I don't think that's going to happen any time soon," said Gretel.

"No," said Jenny. "It's a pretty big crack . . . and it's getting bigger!!!"

As we watched, the ground continued to fracture until the crack reached the stairs of the building we were in.

"Uh-oh," said Roberta. "Time to get going."

Everyone jumped up, grabbed me, and dragged me down the corridor past Mrs Plaster's room and outside.

It was just in time.

As the ground underneath the building continued to crack, the building began shaking and crumbling, and then finally collapsed in a pile of rubble.

We looked around for somewhere else to hide.

The only building left standing was the

building where our classroom was. But it didn't look like it would be there for much longer.

It too was beginning to break up.

Tiles were falling off the roof.

Bricks were being shaken loose.

The whole building began listing to one side and then collapsed in a cloud of dust that enveloped us like a thick fog.

We were coughing and spluttering.

As the dust settled, however, we saw a light.

It was the red light shining from the top of Grantbot's antenna as it advanced towards us.

"Come on!" said Gretel, tugging at my arm.

"No," I said, shaking my arm free.

I knew what I had to do.

The Grantbot was programmed to exterminate enemy robots.

In the Grantbot's eyes, I was an enemy robot.

It had already destroyed the school looking for me. What would be next? The town of Northwest? Central City? The entire world?

Only I had the power to stop it.

"Go and join the rest of the school," I said to my friends.

They all looked at me, stunned.

"Henry!" said Jenny, grabbing at my arm.

"You're not going to do anything stupid, are you?"

"It's too late for that," I said, shaking her off. "If I hadn't been stupid enough to think that Roberta was a robot in the first place, none of this would have happened. It's all my fault, but I'm going to fix it . . . I promise."

Chapter 42

Thief to the rescue

I walked towards the Grantbot.

Its antenna was pulsing brightly.

I shut my eyes.

It would all be over in a moment.

The Grantbot was programmed to destroy robots.

Well, I was the only robot around here. Once it had neutralized me it would stop. Nothing – and nobody – else could be harmed.

It raised its enormous arms in the air. It was going to crush me like a bug.

I braced myself.

That's when I heard the dogs.

Howling, baying and barking.

I opened my eyes.

An enormous pack of dogs, led by Thief, was running towards me.

Well, I soon realized it wasn't so much

towards me, as towards the Grantbot.

The whole pack of dogs – hundreds of them, it seemed – swarmed around the Grantbot's powerful legs. It tried to walk through the pack, but they were jumping up at it in such numbers and with such enthusiasm that they tripped it up and knocked it to the ground.

Then they leaped on top of it, pawing and yelping and licking in a mad frenzy.

The others rushed to my side.

"What's happening, Grant?" I said. "Where did all the dogs come from?"

"I think it's the high-frequency robot-signal jammer," he said. "I told you that dogs could hear it!"

"And they REALLY like it!" said Jenny.

The Grantbot was covered in dog slobber. Plumes of steam and smoke were rising from its shell.

"Uh-oh," said Grant. "Their drool must be getting into the wiring. Stand back . . . this could be dangerous!"

We backed away as the Grantbot hissed and sparked, popped, and then blew apart in a huge explosion that sent dogs flying in all directions.

They hit the ground and ran off, yelping in fright, their tails tucked between their legs.

All that remained of the Grantbot were twisted sheets of metal, nuts, bolts, wires and one shredded boot.

Chapter 43

Mr Brainfright's big idea

We stood there looking at the smoking pile of rubble that had once been our school.

Jenny squeezed my hand. "Don't feel bad, Henry," she said.

"But it's all my fault!" I said. "I am *so* sorry, Roberta."

"It's OK," she said. "You obviously have a *really good* imagination."

"So do you," I said. "That was some story you wrote! You sure had me fooled."

"It wasn't that good," said Roberta. "I didn't have to use much imagination to write it. Mr Brainfright said to write about something that we know, so that's what I did."

Newton gasped. "You really *are* a robot?"

"No," said Roberta. "But I know what it's like to feel *different*. This is the third school I've been to in three years. I always have trouble fitting in. So I really wanted it to work this time. But I guess I've been trying a bit too hard."

"And I guess we haven't exactly made it any easier for you, have we?" I said.

Roberta shrugged. "That's OK," she said. "I kind of feel like we're friends now ... right?"

"You bet!" I said.

"*Best* friends!" said Jenny.

"You are definitely part of the gang now," said Gretel, grinning. "And I'm ready for a rematch any time you are."

"You're on," said Roberta. "It was probably just a fluke that I beat you the other day."

"Well, this has worked out really well for everyone, hasn't it?" said Jack. "And the best thing is *no* school! This is the best day ever!"

"For you maybe," said Jenny. "But not for poor Mr Greenbeard."

Mr Greenbeard was on his knees, his head in his hands.

I think he was crying.

Seeing Mr Greenbeard so upset made me feel even worse than I already did.

At that moment the sun came out and a rainbow arched through the sky over the

175

school. It was kind of sad and beautiful at the same time.

Mr Brainfright knelt beside Mr Greenbeard and clapped his arm around his shoulder. "You know, Mr Greenbeard," he said, "this may be a blessing in disguise – a wonderful opportunity! We can rebuild the school bigger and better than it was before. We can get the students to help – doing is learning, after all."

You could see Mr Brainfright was getting more and more excited about the idea, the more he thought about it.

"We could base our classes around the whole project!" he went on. "Just imagine it. Measuring and calculating – that's maths. The wiring and plumbing – science! And while they're learning about building, they'll also be building their vocabulary – that's English taken care of. They'll be getting plenty of outdoor exercise, so there will be no need for separate sports classes, and they can sing and whistle while they work, which will not only help to pass the time but will add to their musical appreciation."

Mrs Rainbow, who was nodding enthusiastically at Mr Brainfright's speech, went to stand beside him. "I think it's a wonderful idea," she said to Mr Greenbeard. "The children would learn so much from the designing, painting and decorating of the new school. And, who knows, perhaps we could even design the school in the shape of a ship!"

At the mention of the word "ship", Mr Greenbeard looked up and smiled. He got to his feet. "A ship!" he said. "Why yes! Of course! We can build a new, better school ... one that's truly seaworthy. We'll have it shipshape in no time. We'll win that Tidiest School Award next year, you see if we don't!"

Grant stepped forward and said to Mr Greenbeard, "I could build a school-building robot to help with the heavy lifting if you'd like."

"NO!" we all cried at the same time.

Grant looked hurt. "What about a system of pulleys then?" he asked. "I could rig up a block and tackle. Would that be all right?"

"Would it involve robotics of any sort?" asked Mr Greenbeard.

"No, just ropes and wheels," said Grant. Then he added hopefully, "But it could involve a super-advanced digital electronic processing unit if you'd like."

"I think just ropes and wheels will do fine,"

said Mr Greenbeard firmly. "Let's keep it simple."

"Yes, sir," said Grant, sighing. "Just ropes and wheels it is, then."

Chapter 44

Epilogue

Well, that's my story.

And, just in case you're wondering, it's all true.

Every last bit.

If you're ever passing through Northwest, and you happen to be passing Northwest Southeast Central School, feel free to drop in.

We're pretty easy to find. Our school is the one that looks like a ship.

Our classroom is up on the second level, starboard side – the one with extra-big portholes.

Just don't forget to get a life jacket from Mrs Rosethorn at the purser's office . . . we haven't struck any icebergs yet, but – as Jenny's mother always says – it's better to be safe than sorry.

And if you see any robots, don't worry: it will

probably just be us making a film version of Roberta's story. She was so impressed by my costume that she asked me to star in it.

It's going to be a riot!

Read more of

Henry McThrottle's hilarious adventures...

"A rip roaring school story... you're setting
sail for child heaven. A goldmine of fun."
Daily Mail

"A perfectly PG-certificate adventure,
everything is spot on"
Bookbag

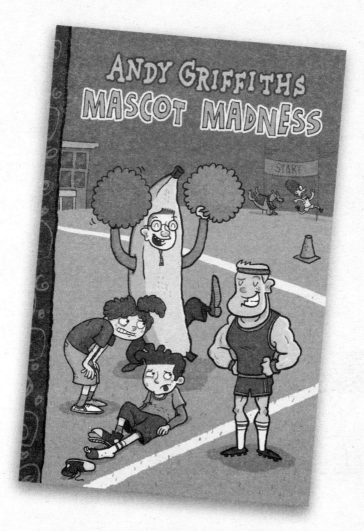

Henry's class go MASCOT MAD in the
funniest sports day in history!